Ella S. Youngs

Paphus

And Other Poems

Ella S. Youngs

Paphus
And Other Poems

ISBN/EAN: 9783337241858

Printed in Europe, USA, Canada, Australia, Japan

Cover: Foto ©Andreas Hilbeck / pixelio.de

More available books at **www.hansebooks.com**

PAPHUS

AND OTHER POEMS

BY

ELLA SHARPE YOUNGS

LONDON
KEGAN PAUL, TRENCH & CO., 1, PATERNOSTER SQUARE
1882

TO VAUGHAN.

I HAVE no costly spikenard of sweet song
In which to embalm thy name, my well-beloved !
That the rich perfume bearing it along,
Through the drear paths of Life, might there have proved
How dear thou wert; but just a simple note,
For thine own unexacting spirit-ear,
Which Love, sweet Sister, on its wings would bear
Unto thee—if so be that Spirits hear—
If so be that from realms, where music bars
The limits, and beats golden time to stars,
A fragment of Earth's song to thee may float,
And thou, pausing, in regions far remote,
Shouldst still thy harp, to catch the faltering rhyme,
Which used to please thee when thou wert of Time.

I would have kept this garden of my Song
With thy dear name o'erflowering it, that there
That lily blooming fragrant, pure and fair,
Might have made all the breezes so ; but strong
Winds of tempestous Thought, and thundrous shower
Born of Imagination's lurid cloud,
Have swept athwart with murmurs swift, and loud,
And rained their shadows round the cherished flower
And weed-wise grown about it,—not for long,
For should this garden stand awhile, thou knowest
That all who love thee will uproot those weeds,
Dissevering them from thy dear name and deeds ;
And, flinging them aside, will gently throng
About thee, lily, wheresoe'er thou growest.

And when the garden is deserted, those
Will risk the o'erhanging brambles, and will climb,
Across the thorns of many a 'wildering rhyme,
To reach thee where thou shinest in repose,
To drink the beauty from that name of thine,
To feel the influence of thy calm fair light,
(As one stoops through the darkness of the night
For the dim fragrance of the eglantine),
Ev'n though the weeds trail closely o'er their feet,
Ev'n though the thorns run sharp beneath their hand ;
For they perchance will feel and understand
How those intruders sprung around thee, sweet !
From out the erratic soil which was to be
Free from all growth, save only thine, and thee.

CONTENTS.

———•◦•———

PAPHUS.

From Tempe's vale arose the mournful sighing
Of Paphus, for a dryad nymph who grew
Faint in the shelter of her guardian oak,
Whose roots beneath *his* curse were blasted dying,
Who garlanded by olive-wreaths and dew,
Smiled on Olympus, and his earlier haunts forsook.

In vain the many vessels wrought, and brazen,
Hung in the branches of the wavering trees ;
No more the oracles of Zeus were bruited
There as of yore, though priests stood by to blazon
His god-like will—no fiats on the breeze,
Shook through the sacred oaks, to speeches faint and
      fluted.

Then weary of their futile task, and well-nigh
Despairing, to Zeus' altar hied the crowd,
With heifers, goats, and acorns interceding,

B

And, hanging on the speeches of the Helli,
   They sought an answer,—then, from out his cloud
Spake Zeus (or thundered), to his people meekly pleading:

   " One of the sacred oaks has whispered speeches
   My mighty lips had never breathed to it,
   And it must die!" Then wept the multitude.
   The consecrated boughs of oaks and beeches
   Waved in a tumult, ere they joined and knit
Their prayer aright—"*Which* tree in all the circling
      wood ?"

   " The third that stands beside the swift Peneus,"
   Came the reply.   Forthwith the people thronged,
   Armed with all implements and weapons rural,
   To work the sentence of offended Zeus
   Upon it; much they toiled and delved and pronged,
As though the structure were hand-fashionèd or mural.

   Full many days they took to cleave the soil,
   Ere the firm roots could be disclosed or bared,
   Like Titan nerves, threading the earthy flesh.
   The labour much their strength did waste and spoil;
   Yet was this neither basely grudged nor spared,
And the fourth week still found them labouring afresh,--

When Zeus, from out the skies, who had beheld
Their travail in his cause, did pity them,
And cried, " My curse alight upon the roots ! "
Then, from the lowest soil the life upwelled
Unaided, and did wither with the stem,
Leaves, trunk, and bark and all, with their unfolding fruits.

But so it chanced, that long ere Zeus had curst
The tree, young Paphus, wand'ring by, had caught
Sight of the nymph who dwelt within it safe,
And whose bright beauty from its life was nurst ;
(As spirit might find dwelling in a thought),
And much his flexile heart did ponder this and chafe.

'Twas when the nymph had in the dawning slipt
From her dim covert, to the neighb'ring wave,
To newly dew each fine and curvèd limb ;
Ere she had yet unloosed her zone and dipt :
Paphus came floating down the tide, and gave
Her love-born looks which she, blushing, returned to him.

He was a Phrygian prince, and much had seen,
In his far court, of beauty ; but hers was
A gem new shining up from mines undreamt.
And very fair she must have seemed I ween,
Unconscious of life's ways and frigid laws,
With deep dark eyes like Night's, and golden hair
unkempt,

And rosy lights along her limbs which grew
Like moonshine in the waters ; for the fresh
And winding waves soon claspt her, and did throw
Their pure green shadows o'er her like a dew,
Circling in mirroring eddies round her flesh,
Which soon one tender grey and hyaline did grow.

She struck white arms athwart the pressing foam,
She laught with Fancy's glee, and did pursue
Flowers and winging fish down the free tide :
Then turned anew to Paphus, who did home
His eyes within her form, and who did sue,
At her most innocent mouth, boons that were undenied.

They laught and kist through dawning, till a beam
Shot gold and green upon them from the boughs :
When suddenly the dryad blushed and cried,
" The Sun ! the Sun !" and bounding from the stream,
Pursued by Paphus and his fiery vows,
Within that guardian oak her trembling limbs did hide.

And there, grief-tortured, did the Phrygian prince
Thro' day and night (until the rapturous dawn
Gave back his nymph unto him) his love-song
Outpour unceasingly ; and ever since
His steps had wandered restless and forlorn
Beside that oak, which held his love in sheath so strong.

The Helli, seeing him by night and day
   Clasp the old tree and murmur mystic prayers,
Spake, " Lo! he questioneth the oracle!
Let him alone—the good alone can pray;
   Let him alone—he may be, unawares,
Some offspring of the gods." Thus Paphus farèd well.

They brought him fruits and flowers, offerings,
   Incense, and oak-wreaths; and his solitude
Was otherwise as deep as Grief can love.
Shaken alone by Love's melodious wings,
   And the maid's voice, who in the tree did brood
On all he spoke in sighs—and much he sighed not of.

For she was nurst on winds and waters; gleams
   Of sunshine, and most mystic moonlight fare;
These were her loved and earliest ministers.
But as some radiant world bursts on our dreams,
   So Paphus came to hers, and taught her there
Were other worlds and loves, more beautiful than hers.

Perchance it was Love's poison in the oak
   Which made it whisper false when Zeus declared
His oracles—we know that Love is death.
And now the launchèd arrow flew, and broke
   Its venom in the bosoms that were bared
Unto it, and that held no antidote beneath.

When Paphus learnt the doom that must befall
The guardian of a hundred years, and her
For whom his life was wasting, in affright
He summoned from his realm his courtiers all,
And warriors with all trusty arms that were
Vowed his, if haply *they* might shield it with their might.

But all their strength united, and their arms
Can not avail against the people's rage.
" What, Zeus offended ? he might strike with plague,
Or drought, or famine ! "   Thus their strange alarms
They vent in strokes redoubled, to assuage
The ire they dread, which still unthreat'ning is, and
vague.

Round Paphus stand his followers with faces
Rueful, to view the fearful work advance,
Strengthless the Grecian numbers to resist.
Axes, and hammers, halberds, blades and maces
Royal and rural weapons, strike and glance,
In the south hours, and strive the oak's firm limbs to
twist.

Which groan, and crack, as though each stroke dis-
severed
A life, and much does Paphus hope and fear
For her who lies i' the heart, foredoomed and weeping,

The dryad of the tree ; he has endeavoured
To save the life which is so doubly dear   .
Unto him, now that its young pulse with fear is leaping.

It was a moonlight evening when they smote
Their latest blow, and left the spot till dawn,
Rejoicing that the tree should with it die.
Each moonbeam floated, an ethereal boat
With sails dream-filled, and gentle motion born
Of Night and Love, which winged it through the tideless
     sky.

They left ; but Paphus knelt against the trunk,
Doomed to its death with morning's earliest ray,
And prayed his love to save their life in flight,
And with his tears the soft night winds were drunk.
His prayer resisted Diōne alway :
" Leave me to death," she cried ; " Love has no saving
     might !

Love has no might to save, ev'n could I bend
This bark at midnight and come forth to thee :
If we could reach earth's limits, I must die—
Must die beloved.   My fate doth ever blend
With this my faithful shelterer's : we shall be
One in our deaths, and ne'er apart dissevered lie.

Thou art but mortal—I immortal am
In spirit, and this shrine immortal is ;
Our forms may strew the earth, but still we live
Elsewhere for ever." Thus her accents swam
Out on the moonbeams to him ; but a bliss
Crept through his frame, which taught he still must weep
      and strive.

He wept aloud. Within the bark there grew
Silence a space. Beside him a soft foot
Winged on the white airs. Gazing, he descried
Zeus' foam-born offspring, like a midnight dew,
Pallid and swift, who, pausing at the root,
Heard all his grief, then moved to tender pity, cried—

" Diōne, thee I loose ! The Soul of Love
Bids thee reply to Love's most amorous breath."
The rugged stem oped up and let her through,
And Paphus with new bliss he dreamt not of,
Along Peneus to elude stern Death,
Through the long night and chill with his fair dryad
      flew.

They tarried not for rocks, all chasms stemmed,
And, gliding down the liquid channels went ;
Leaping with aërial steps o'er the deep rifts,

And, leaving then the tide all foam-begemmed,
  Up Ossa's thyme-dressed sides their footsteps bent,
And reached a sheltered cave within the mountain clefts,

  Where Paphus laid his forest-maid asleep,
  While he watched for that dawn, which should have
      been
  Her death-hour ; in the triumph of his love.
  He fanned with tender gaze her slumbers deep,
  And stood 'twixt her and Fate—a mortal screen—
And thought her safe from harm : and safe she was
      enough

  From mortal ills; but when in Tempe's plain
  The tree fell, shivered by the Helli's hate,
  And Silence drew her breath above the stroke,
  They watched some sign from Zeus, and watched in
      vain.
  " Had they not striven his sacred wrath to sate ;
Was he still pitiless?"   'Twas thus their wailings broke.

  But Zeus was unpropitiated ; he
  Knew that the soul was fled from out that stem
  Ere it was yielded : so his anger grew,
  And storms he meted out imperiously
  Unto the people of that vale ; to them
Moreover he did speak, in thunderings anew.

He told them *where* the Spirit of that tree
Was wand'ring unpursued, and bade them follow,
Armed with his mandate for its hasty death.
Ere Tempe's vale had echoed the decree,
The people started, headed by Apollo,
Their god's sweet son, who cleared their pathway by his
       breath.

And Ossa's wooded heights, and ere long Pelion's
Were echoes to their murderous feet, and soon
They gained the cavern where Dĩone slept,
Guarded by Somnus and his mystic sons,
Dreams, soft as Love's own glance beneath a moon
Which with her lover o'er the nymph its vigil kept.

The night was calm as a Sleep-shrouded sea
Whose waves float Light upon a boundless shore,
And the still Hours reclined, like sleeping sprites,
On cradling breezes, which crept dreamily
Over the mountains.   Life seemed ebbed and o'er,
And nought was wakeful there, save Love's deep eye, and
       Night's.

More fairylike the dryad seemed in sleep,
Than waking ever saw her.   Her smooth limbs
Were folded flower-wise, and closed her palms

Like petals fallen when the day was deep
In drowsiness.   We know how moonlight dims
In its ethereal veil, and beautifies such charms.

She slumbered on, her waxen lids close-prest,
With kissing lashes on her checks' round bloom,
And lips apart, while tender sighs burst through
As fragrance from a flower, and each breast
Seem'd a curved mirror, flashing through the gloom,
The moon's white radiance back, beneath the mid-
　　night dew.

Even Apollo paused beside the oak
That shaded o'er the cavern's portal, while
His godlike features glanced to gentleness
A moment ere upon such dreams he broke.
He paused, and pitifully 'gan to smile
As he stepped forth to lead his followers to success.

Then on the cavern's silence burst the Helli
With fiery wrath, and the pursuing crowd ;
Demanding Paphus' life, and the pale dryad's,
Who, leaping from her slumbers, eyed the Selli
With looks that wept for clemency aloud,
And prayers that seemed the speech of waterfalls, or
　　naïads'.

In vain—they thronged around the trembling pair
With weapons lifted, and triumphant cry,
Then flew Diōne to the sheltering tree
Beside the cave, and, kneeling there in prayer,
She clasped smooth arms, wrought pale with agony,
Around it.   "Thou who oft before hast sheltered me,

Take to thy core two lovers.   Keep us fast
As thy most sacred bark *can* hold," she cried.
"Oh! fail me not in this most deadly hour!
And, as thou would'st each storm and scathe outlast
Wherefrom thy kith and kin may die, have died,
Stretch o'er this youth I love thy supernatural power."

'Tis said the Oak was moved, and acorns fell
Like tears from its strange rustling, while the bark
Worked slowly, but most steadily apart.
"Lo!" cried the people, "she hath wrought a spell!"
"Hush!" cried the Helli, "Zeus is speaking, hark!
His mighty voice comes down straight through this oaken
    heart."

They paused a moment to foresee the end
Of this strange miracle: Diōne clung
To the grey trunk with one arm, while the other
Grew circlingly around her Phrygian friend,
Whose love about *her* like an armour hung,
Though each was a defence, defenceless to the other.

The hoary stem went slowly opening, and
The dryad peeped with shadow-laden eyes,
Into the hollow bark, which like a womb
Parted to take her in : she thrust a hand
Into the cleft, and soon with glad surprise
They saw her pierce entire through the unwonted tomb.

But when her Paphus she essayed to draw
Into the fissure after her sweet self,
The wound began to close tumultuously.
Then, when her lover's perilous fate she saw,
Left to the murderous throng, the dryad-elf
Strove much to join him, but around her grew the tree.

Slowly one rugged hollow, moss-grown layer
Grew on another. The white nymph within
Prayed for escape or to rejoin her lover
In vain : the oak was dumb and weak the prayer.
In vain did Paphus rend and bruise his skin
To keep the cleft apart; it closed the dryad over,

Whose pallid face was as a sinking star,
While with her terror-stricken eyes she kist,
Her love, in ling'ring farewell glances cast
About him. Oh ! those eyes' hot kisses are,
What least a lover's spirit may resist !
And his was waxing faint within him, dim and fast.

Yet woman-wise her eyes she would not veil
With lids closed o'er their pain, nor even dim
With tears, so long as she could see her love.
The closer grew the bark, deeper the wail
That mutely rent her gaze for love of him.
Such grief might well appease the Fate it strove to move.

The Helli seeing how the oak had bared
Its bosom to the Spirit of the oak,
And left lorn Paphus to his fate and woes,
Cried, "Ho, the culprit, slay him ! We have spared
His life too long !"   Then full their fury broke
Upon him, and he fell, pierced through by shafted throes.

They left him there, and turned them to the vale
Whence their young god-like leader did uproot
His laurel, for the Pythian shrines preferred.
And the still air bore on its balmy gale
The death-plaint of their victim, that sole fruit
Of his most fatal love : and Evening came and heard.

And woe ! his oak-interred Diōne held
Her fluttering heart to catch his latest breath,
As it came floating through the healèd bark
In evening's silent hours: and when there swelled
The sea of clouds like billows from beneath
To ebb in the sky's ocean, and when through the dark

Heav'n should have glowed with Light-sparks which
    the breath
Of Nyx sends floating in those myriad stars
That quiver at each inhalation drawn,
Lo ! a stern tempest rioting like death,
And dealing to the mountains fearful scars,
Scathing their oaken sons, and killing life till dawn.

It was th' avenging rage of Zeus, for he
Launched in the lightning's swift and sweeping hand
The bolt which slew the oak that sheltered her
Whom he pursued—Diōne helplessly
Fell as a night-swept leaf upon the land
In that stupendous storm which Ossa's roots did stir.

She fell on Paphus' scarcely chillèd corpse,
And they lay in a tender heap, for Day
To gaze on with its unrelenting eye.
Death spared her loveliness, who soils and warps
The beauty he has snatched from Life away,
To feed his evil glance to dread satiety.

But it is spoken in pale whispers round,
That a twin Spirit-light, betwixt the hours
Of darkness flits and prays about the spot ;
And clenches in dumb agony the ground,
And wrestles fearfully, with voiceless powers
Of Ill—and thus are shunned the blasted oak and grot.

And that all night pale arms and blood-stained breast
(Wherein a gory fount seems never dry)
Shine like sad meteors all the darkness in.
Which ev'ry passing eye has since confest,
And if one yearn the sight, one must draw nigh
At evening and nightfall, to Pelion's sacred twin,

And there outwatch the light, when, with a groan
A phantom oak breaks haplessly in twain,
Wherefrom a star-white dryad leaps to death.
But if one be to lore and legend prone,
'Twere best to leave the husk around the grain,
Nor sift it into Truth, lest sooth there lie beneath.

FLORENCE, *November*, 1881.

SUNBEAMS.

WE float in the van
Of the Titan-born,
When his fiery span
Divides the dawn,
And the young clouds blush
At his chariot's touch,
And the pulsing air
Scatters its dew on the breast of Morn
Everywhere !
Since his sire's birth
From the womb of Earth,
No god has laughed
In the face of Time,
No mortal quaffed
From the spheres sublime
More merrily than he !
Hark ! to the crash
Of his chariot wheels,
As they hotly dash
On the leaden heels
Of Night, which wearily,

Lags on the mountain crests and clouds,
Weighs on the ocean's ashy shrouds,
   As a mist below which we,
Pierce into spokes of golden light
Chase to the confines of daylight,
     Speedily !

    We weave the robe
    Which the Hours wear,
    When they float the globe,
    When they cleave the air,
On wings with our radiance freighted.
    And Eōs ties,
    O'er her blinded eyes,
(Blind with her brother's splendour
And the blaze of his chariot weighted)
    The buds which we
    Ope fragrantly
With our viewless hands and tender.
    While Hyperion sits
    Where her white train flits,
From the marge of Oceanus' water,
    And smiles to think
    How its girding brink
Fades from his cloud-cleaving daughter.

    When the day grows hot,
    And the young god's wheel

Revolveth not,
We swiftly steal
To the shadowy green
Of some ocean nest,
And glide unseen
To the wave-washed breast,
Of the floating Oceanides.
How the water cleaves,
Like wind-blown leaves,
When each snowy limb
Grows pale and dim
'Neath the billows that divide us !
For with virgin arms
They fly our charms,
And the weltering waves deride us :
But we pursue
Through the woof of blue,
Till the shades of the sea-depths hide us ;
Then we tremble back
On our surging track,
And dry our wings in heaven,
Till his steeds uprise
To career the skies,
And the young god's shout is given.
When day is no more
We press on before
To open the gates of Nyx,

Which we hold ajar,
With a silver star,
While the shadows kiss and mix.
Then we spread our cloak
Of a crimson dye,
Where the sun-steeds broke
Their race on high,
And the god steps out
With triumphal shout
To his palace in the West,
While each panting steed
Is led to feed,
In the islands of the Blest.

MOONBEAMS.

We breathe and wake
On the bosom white
Of some sleeping lake,
As lilies fair
Dream in a snowy light.
We gently tread
Where the outlines red
Of sun-clouds fell before,
Flakes on the slumbering air.

When Selene springs
With new-girt wings
Through the gloomy arch of Time,
We lay light fingers
Where shadow lingers,
And silver it into rime.
From the billowy shore
Of the sea above,
We calm the roar
With a kiss of love,
And the clouds divide and sever.
Then we toss its spray
To left and right,
Where the Milky Way
Unfolds in light,
And gathers it up forever !

One night from afar
Came an unloved star,
And Diana her glance o'ershrouded.
With the skin of a lion,
The hunter Orion
Our firmament o'erclouded.
Then the son of Astræus,
By virtue of Zeus,
Uprose with the goddess to plead.
A tear, as she listened,
On her eyelid glistened,

She heard and revoked the deed.
   Then the stars came out
   With a voiceless shout
Of melody unimprisoned,
   And a throne afar
   To the Hunter-star
Was granted as Hesperus' meed.

   We Virgins tread
   The draperies spread
For the foot of the silent Night.
   And stars (unproven
   To earth) have woven
Us paths of shadowless light !
   So we float the spheres
   In revolving tiers,
And the son of Chaos bendeth.
   When our dreamy gaze,
   Through his shadowy maze,
To its farthest verge descendeth.
   Then with step of snow
   We pass below,
To where Uranus binds
   His sons from their birth;
   While their mother, Earth,
Weeps to the wandering winds.

THE HOURS.

From the limits of Creation,
We, Creation's after-birth,
Smiling o'er our new formation,
Clasping glowing hands in mirth,
Trod the viewless winds and waters,
To the eye unseen—unheard,
Ether's light and tameless daughters
In a race both swift and weird.
From our footfalls flowers are springing,
Seeds of bitterness spring too,
Souls are waking, souls are winging,
Shades are born, and sunbeams singing,
Dust is treading down the dew !
And the portals of existence
Swinging are on unseen axis,
Human hearts in mute resistance
With dread Atrōpos, and Lachesis.
Time our father, Time our slayer,
To our steps unwearying cleaves,
And, unheeding prayers or prayer,
Binds us in his withered sheaves.
We are spirits twelve in number,
Gird the Earth, and Air, and Sea,

Twelve in waking, twelve in slumber,
Doubling joy and misery,
Till our shrouds are cast around us,
And our father's hand has wound us
In the unawaking cerements of a dark Eternity.

ETERNITY.

Who calls as a voice of waters athwart a storm of grief?
Flowers are sere and over, withered the bud and the
    bloom,—
I gather them swiftly to me with the life-downtrodden
    leaf,
And bind the quiv'ring tendrils in the silence of the tomb.
Come! for Time is dying, and his locks are grey and thin;
Soon my gates must open for his furrowed frame and heart,
Safely stored for ever when his footstep once is in
The threshold: now he holds us widely, wearily apart.
Sunbeams flicker round earth's cradles, moonbeams kiss
    its silent biers,
Life and Death clasp ready hands across the exodus of
    Time ;
And my arm is waiting, raised to still the motion of the
    spheres,

But I pause awhile to listen, what *the Will* above me
    saith,
The new life within my womb strives to its first exulting
    chime,
And I see on swift dark pinions, drawing nigh the death
    of Death.

FLORENCE, *June*, 1880.

SERENATA.

I HAVE sung at thy window, sweet !
As the bird to the ev'ning star ;
I have paused for the echoes fleet,
Of thy voice at every bar.
The chords of my mandoline
Have thrilled to the touch I brought,
For my love was woven with each line,
Like a warm and living thought.
Stoop, sweet ! and say
To me thy vesper prayer,
Love will shrive thee any day,
Love, which ascends the live-long night
To thee, as a flower's breath to light,
    Unaware !

I have sung of all sweet things
But of *thee* have said no word,—
The spirit that sweeps through the yielding strings
Must be sooner *felt* than heard.
So my love as it breathes in song
Must enshrine thee in no name

But the melody that rolls along
Like a silver spirit-flame.
Come to me, love !
Lean over the sill ;
I will *feel* thee there,
As I gaze above,
Through the dewy night and still,
   Unaware !

I have bid night-buds, and stars,
Weave around thee like a cloud.
I have set no rigid bars
On the love that leaps aloud
In a heart that fainting swims
Through an ocean of deep bliss,
Till it spreads its flagging limbs
In the warmth of a spirit-kiss !
Linger no longer,
Where thou'rt leaning down
The sill, at my prayer,—
For the wind grows stronger,
The blue night shades are growing brown,
   Unaware.

Tinkling the strings are, faint and low ;
And my hand drops off to a pensive rest,
I have run the measures so soft and slow,
To beat with the life in thy sleeping breast,

Which falls and rises, which ebbs and flows,
Through thy parted lips in a wavering breath,
As a midnight breeze o'er the mouth of the rose
Might swell and droop in the path beneath.
I kiss thee, love !
Where thou dreaming art,
So helpless, and so wondrous fair,
On thy innocent pillow above,
As a closed thought on the heart,
   Unaware !

FLORENCE, *May*, 1881.

TO ——.

"Though passion's trance is overpast,
    Since tenderness and truth outlast
    And live, whilst all wild feelings keep
    Some mortal slumber dark and deep,
    I will not weep—I will not weep!"

OUR love should be a book long closed, and claspt and
    put away;
But Mem'ry sometimes takes it down, from off the shelf of
    Time,
And the breath of the old spirit blows the dust from the
    decay,
And those unforgotten hours shine out like silver thoughts
    in rhyme.
Then my fingers wand'ring go betwixt the leaves, and here
    and there,
Find a flow'r prest (oh, so lovingly!), its fragrance like a
    shade,—
Just some tiny star of summer, or a spray of maidenhair,
Growing pale as parted hearts are, or as buds in shadowy
    glade,—
            And the pride and the pain,
            Of our parting come again,
O'er a spirit which has lived its life, and died all unafraid,

Love was loved and Life was lived for us, in one brief
    summer's day
(All the sweetness of two spirits, concentrated in one
    hour !).
Was it not too much to hope and think such bliss could
    last alway ?
If it could, are human hearts so strong they might outlive
    its power ?
Oh, my love, we blasted life with Passion's swift and fiery
    breath !
Oh, my love, we garnered sorrow in our soul's first fatal
    tryst !
Though the coil of living bind us, our poor hearts are
    numbed to death,
And we stretch despairing spirit-hands, for sunshine through
    the mist,
           But Life's mist strikes chill,
           Turn where'er we will,
As if some spectre of the tomb, seized those weak hands
    and kist.

We might each return to-morrow to the heart each has
    forsworn,
We might catch a faint reflection of spent passion through
    the gloom,
But shall love again enthrall us as _that_ love when it was
    born ?
Can we fill the flower's chalice with its scattered perfume ?

Could we go on living alway, with our spirits near the
    sun,
While the dust of earth grew wearily about our lagging
    feet?
While the wheel of Life ran on, we two should find we
    could not run,
Side by side for ever as at first, in a harmony com-
    plete.
            If we could not ever
            Love, and not dissever,
It were better to break living off, while loving yet were
    sweet.

I should not reach this closèd book from Time's o'er-
    shadowed shelf,
And turn o'er the well-loved pages, and kiss o'er each
    faded bud ;
For the Memory brings on me but soul-scorning of my-
    self,
And the pain is all too fearful for weak heart of woman-
    hood.
I send thee just one leaf beloved, o'erwritten with thy
    name,
The ink scarce dried upon't ; the blots (forgive them) were
    heart tears,

Wrung for one brief moment only.   Read—then cast into
  the flame
This remembrance of one hour fled with the long-departed
  years.

> Then set thy troubled heart,
> In love, from love to part,

Which embitters all existence, for the moment that it
  cheers.

I have closed the book, and look my life once more full
  in the face.
'Tis *so* brief, and after-living is so long, and we may find,
In a higher life, our passion springing up from root of
  grace,
With the time and sphere to culture it unto an even
  mind.
Heav'n is love, and Earth is passion, spirit ether, clay our
  dust ;
Passion is the dross, and love the gold,—it must be purged
  with fire ;
Though the furnace be thrice-heated, we must pass it
  through, *we must,*
And the metal of pure Love shall come out shining from
  Desire.

> In a calm fair sphere above,
> Where God is enthroned in love,

And our spirits in their flight shall soar for ever high,
  and higher.

RAINBOW SONG.

When the skies are alive with the storm,
  And the Earth lifts her faltering mouth,
(Which the lightnings have smitten with warm
  Quick white desolation of drouth),
To the shower that comes quickly, and thickly,
  The sunbeams glance in on the shower,
Then wreathing my storm-colours quickly
  Together, I leap into flower.
        Mingling and weaving,
        Glancing and cleaving,
Catching the rain and sundrops, like gems where the
        twinklingly fall.
        Shifting and heaving,
        The dim vapours sieving,
I laugh on the mist-wreaths, and climb the cloud-wall.

The nymphs of the winds, and the naiads,
  Come dipping their wings in my tide,
Where the seven sweet hues, like the Pleiads,
  Encoil and dissolve side by side.

                              D

The storm lifts me up into heaven,
   The rain flails me back toward earth,
And ere half my life has been given,
   Men mourn o'er the death of my birth.
      The ether enfolds me,
      The sun-radiance golds me,
While the tempest unbinds with a touch, the swathe of my
        chrysalis-bands.
      The vapour remoulds me,
      The firmament holds me,
A tissue of water and air in its hands !

Yet I reign through the ether, and mountain,
   And drop from the hem of a cloud,
And play like an aërial fountain,
   In coloured sprays leaping aloud.
Each breath of the West wind can curve me,
   Each vapour can change me, and yet
The elements tarry to serve me,
   And from pole to far pole I am set
      For the storm, as a bridge,
      O'er whose airy ledge,
It strides to mid-heav'n in endeavour to save its dark foot
        from the flood.
      And the wind, like a sedge
      Sweeps along to its edge,
Like a soul in pursuit of the body and blood.

I am Spirit of sunbeams and raindrops,
    Or a shrine, where the clouds tempest-driven
Have fled to, and woven to fane-tops,
    For the winging ministers of heaven
To meet in, and worship Creation,
    Whose soul is pent up in my hues,
Which dissolve in a fair exhalation,
    And pass over the earth clad in dews.
        From the storm's woof and weft,
        A shred I am left
Across the white path of the airs, where they stand passion-
        fretted and chill,
        Till the sungleams relift
        Their glances, and sift
Through the skies, the new life in their limitless will.

FLORENCE, *December*, 1881.

MIND-VESPERS.

In Silence' dim cathedral aisle I stood,
And closed the doors of Speech, and soft ideal
Fancies, like white-robed choristers, did steal,
Hither and thither, through my dreamy mood.
These soon broke into anthems of clear Song,
While Incense of sweet aspirations sprung
From my low-kneeling spirit—swift, and strong,
Bright gleams shone down from silver lamps of Hope,
Which in my mind most tremulously hung.
Then, through the shadowed naves, a glorious throng
Of thoughts, like spectres, seemed to pass, and grope
At Mem'ry's portal. . . . Soon white Slumber fell
Across the waving mighty multitude,
Which struck it low as might the Host's sweet triple
    bell.

October, 1881.

IN MEMORIAM.

E. V. Y.

No shadow fell upon the world when thou
Didst leave it—no keen grief, no sighs, no tears
From other hearts than ours : the Earth has biers
Too many, to enwreathe about her brow
The cypress gathered from each grave ; but those
To whom thou wert the sun, and moon, of day
And night, grown dim without thee, even they
Know how the sky looks for its vanished ray,
And how Life's garden despoiled of its rose.

My love, my love ! my more than all—for most
Have treasures scattered here, and there, to love,
Lives, and keen aims, and happiness enough
Diffused in many rays ; but when I lost
Thee in one moment, 'twas as if my soul
Had suddenly been turnèd into void,
And in that wrench had felt itself destroyed :
Swayed by no impulse more, no longer buoyed
By aspirations ; past all hope, or goal.

And when, day after day, I smote the sod
And tried to feel thee through, or see thee smile
In vain, sweet Faith within me changed to vile
Reproaches : " God, what hast Thou done, O God ?
Were other lives not nearer Thee than hers
That Thou shouldst stretch and take her with Thy
    might ?
Hadst Thou in Heav'n too little of Thy light
That Thou didst take her thus into Thy sight?"
Christ pardon me ! if thus I raved and worse.

But when the peace and hush of Heav'n came through
Sweet tender memories of thee to this
Rebellious heart, I almost felt thee kiss
Me to submission, and I slowly grew
What thou wouldst have me be ; and though forlorn
The heart which holds a grave, still flow'rs may grow
Of Faith and Patience, to o'erveil the woe
With their white fragrance ; and above the snow
Of my despair, I *am* resignèd, Vaughan !

Only sometimes, when thy belovèd Art
Comes rushing with the old old sweetness o'er
My spirit, and the Classic numbers pour,
In chastened music, through my bursting heart,
Then surges up the unforgotten pain !
I almost see thee winging o'er the notes
Those gifted fingers, and my passion floats

Back on the Stream of Grief in fiery motes,
And I return to what I was, again.

But then the stars thou lovedst come to shine
Through the red Sunset's fingers, like sweet eyes
Gazing from Passion, which averted flies
And I am comforted, for I am thine
Once more in peace ; if only Night could last !
But morrows come with new temptations set
About them, like a thorny coronet,
And Light brings back what Night had made forget,
And thus one lives for ever o'er the Past.

I know that thou art blest, and that thy form
In Earth's kind arms takes tender sleep ; I know
The Sea's slow requiem goes, with ebb and flow
About thee, and the Olives weave their warm
Soft traceries above thee ; yet the eyes
Are dimmed that ply those distant heav'ns to see
If haply, when the clouds rush past, there be
A shade of thy sweet presence there, or thee ;
And Space alone smites back to agonize.

San Remo, *November 27th.*

TO VAUGHAN.

WHEN from some careless lip I hear
That tend'rest name of "Sister" flung,
Life's overshadowed paths among,
Through the world's tumult on my ear,
My heart falls dim with sudden grief,
And tears, that none can see avowed,
Sweep o'er it in a tempest brief,
And thou—thou passest in that cloud.
With pale fair brow, and earnest eyes,
And loving looks, and gentlest ways,
Thy touch the best of sympathies,
Thy smile the sweetest gift of praise.
Oh, love of my most early years !
Oh, guide of my most wayward heart !
Oh, comforter of all those fears
I loved to bring thee, and impart !
Thou more than sister, best of friends,
With all a woman's instinct firm
To succour, and to guide to ends
Most noble, from ignoble germ.
And yet *so* tender thou didst lead
In silken chains the iron-willed,

Thy lips were formed to intercede,
And what they pleaded, was fulfilled.
So true thy love, so pure, so deep
It lay soul-fathoms, none could know
Who saw thee smile, who saw thee weep,
That thou couldst bear and struggle so.
Thy very love gave wondrous strength,
And patience to hope on and wait,
And thou rewarded wast at length,
When Heav'n flung wide its pearl-wrought gate,
And showed what peace and loveliness
Await at that eternal goal
Those, who through Faith their suffering soul
In God-like patience do possess.
Oh ! my beloved, was it all vain
The pain of life, the spirit pain,
The glorious triumphs, and the sweet
Love-deeds, that made thee so complete
To take thy place a little higher,
When Death came winged with God's white fire ?
No, *never* vain ; thou now hast found
That every Cross is doubly crowned
With Light, and that thou hast enough
Of tenderness to give thee rest,
Of blessedness to make thee blest,
Of love, to satisfy *thy* love.

San Remo, *November 27th.*

"FOR SO HE GIVETH HIS BELOVED SLEEP."

(In Memoriam E. V. Y.)

Sleep on, beloved! rest is for those who tire
Of earth in life's first hours—as thou,—and creep
Like weary children just a little higher,
To drop within a Father's arms asleep.
So thou—when life had cast dim Grief around thee,
Didst close thy lids a little while, to weep;
And mourning, fell to slumber, for God found thee,
And gave thee even His beloved's sleep.

He knew not what could soothe thy spirit better
When pain had weighed it unto weariness,
And, breaking from thee that unceasing fetter,
He raised thee in His mighty arms to bless.
And kissed thee through the shadowy vale—that blessing
Lingered within thy death-smile, sweet and deep,
For thou didst feel a benediction pressing
Upon thee, when God gave His loved one sleep.

It was not Death, that gentle exhalation
Of a pure spirit floating into Life;
Here the wild grief, in Heaven the exultation
Of angels, o'er a soul released from strife.
There all the light, if *here* the sod o'er-shrouding
Our vision, from the joys which God doth keep,
Veiled in that glory which He comes unclouding,
When thus He giveth His belovèd sleep.

Sleep safe from sorrow! Thy young soul is standing,
Beside the Crystal Sea, in undreamt bliss,
And peace, that ever passeth understanding,
Which God reserves for spirits that are *His.*
And, tender to the dust He hath created,
He gives it unto Earth awhile to keep
(Until all things be changed and renovated)—
Even so He giveth His belovèd sleep.

San Remo, *November* 27th.

TO THE SPIRIT OF MUSIC.

DAY-STAR of the realms where Thought
Shrinks into itself, and dwindles
Visibly—as glow-worms ought,
When the moon her white light kindles,—
Sweetest Spirit of those hours
When we know immortal powers,
Hover round our souls in trances,
Lit at thy melodious glances,
Weave around me now the web
Of a tide that knows no ebb.

Faint I stand on shores where Silence
Is vibrating like a vision,
But afar, on Sound's white islands,
Pace the winds in glorious mission,
Bearing music's subtle foam
On the waves that curling come
O'er our poet-thoughts, to break
At the Mind's ear, with a Wake.

Spirit reach with soft hands' splendour,
Through the strifes and earthly jars,
To the poet-heart some tender
Minstrelsy, of unborn stars—
Songs that those white choirs at dawning,
Chaunted to the listening Morning,
With pure lip, and deathless throat,
And a *soul* dropt in each note !

Spirit come ! and tread through measures
Light as air thy radiant dance,
Fairest of heav'n's hoarded treasures
To my waking soul advance !
Bring me sounds of many oceans,
Bring me breath of all emotions,
Bring me *Heaven* to inherit
In thy silver hands, sweet spirit !

FLORENCE.

REQUIEM.

SLEEP, loveliest, sleep !
Nought can unseal thine eyes,
On which calm Slumber lies
    Peacefully and deep.
Nought shade the marble-light
Of thy features still and white,
    While we sad vigils keep.

Sleep, fairest and best !
Thou mayst not fear to wake,
Nought evermore can shake
    Thy holy rest ;
Or bid thine eyes unclose
From their flower-like repose.
    We watch thee, loveliest !

Oh ! peaceful be thy dreams,
Of Heav'n and holy things.
Thy soul hath found its wings,
    The moon in silence gleams,

The wave its requiem sings,—
Hushed, holy, calm and deep,
　　Now be thy sleep.

　Sleep, loveliest and best !
Thou wak'st on earth no more,
As thou hast oft before,
　　From slumber's rest ;
But, from thy Home above,
Sweet spirit shed thy love
　　On souls opprest !

SAN REMO, *November 27th.*

ELMĀZA.

THE storm is swelling in the cloud, and weaving many a
        mortal's shroud,
    And purple is the desert rim.
The light sand twirls, then flutters down, like scorchèd
        leaves or moth-wings brown,
    And the day is dim.
Leave not our tent, thou stranger bold : the Simoom's gust
        blows hot and cold,
    On who opposes.
The path is long, the camels breath comes short, as if he
        snorted death,
    And the daylight closes.

HE.

I must away, I spurn delay,
Give me a steed to beat the air,
With hoofs like breezes at their play,
And will to bear me anywhere !
This tent is for bedāwee blood,
The scorching sands for feet like thine,

But oh ! the ocean's restless flood,
And mountain paths were made for *mine !*
Thy tent hath been a grateful screen,
From many a death-stroke of thy sun.
I thank thee for what thou hast been,
I thank thee for what thou hast done,
For ev'ry draught to cool my thirst,
For ev'ry moonlit dance, and song,
'Neath which my heart has leapt, has burst,
(It must not hear, nor feel, too long !).
I shake my rein and I am gone.

SHE.

Nay, stay, and I will bathe thy feet, in water welling
    cool and sweet
    From the well's heart,
And gather dates as rich as those which Siivah's golden
    palms disclose,
    Ere thou depart.
I'll fan thee with the leaves we take, beside the desert's
    emerald lake,
    That oāsis where
Our flocks are pastured and there springs water, thro'
    shade and all cool things
    And unscorched air.
The camels' bells are tinkling fleet, their milk is flowing
    pale and sweet,
    In our cool jars.

E

The Day has wandered far away from Night, and o'er the
        heav'ns there play,
    The first white stars.
And if thou scorn'st a couch so rude as *that* we spread
        in solitude,
    Which yields us rest,
Take (sooner than depart our wild free life) an Arab's
        undefiled
    And passionate breast,
On which to lay thy head, 'twill be a faithful pillow unto
        thee,
    Thou pallid child !

HE.

I may not pause—

SHE.

Not when a maiden—

HE.

My heart with dreams of love is laden !
Her lips, her eyes—Elmāza—

SHE.
Yet

Thou leavest all with no regret !

HE.

Her dusky hair, like clouds that rise
To overshade her haunting eyes
I must away.

SHE.

Whose lip doth burst
And scorch, will he refuse its thirst
When the well bubbles?

HE.

Let me go,

SHE.

And meet thy heart, thy deadliest foe
Alone?

HE

Nay, but our lives divide.

SHE.

Love rides with true love, side by side.

HE.

Thy form which bends beneath a touch
Like a stem, one may not handle much
Lest it should break!

SHE.

And it was made
For Love's own clasp—as hilt for blade.

HE.

Thy voice, Elmāza,—oh! the sea
Has no vibrating harmony
Like that!

SHE.

And it will swell for thee.
Beloved !—although our creed, our name,
Our home, our lineage, our fame
Are bars betwixt this bliss and us,
We love, and are victorious !
Thy cheek is white and mine will grow
'Neath thy dear glance as chaste as snow
(Since snow is pallid as thou sayest).
My home is all this land,—my skiff
The camel tethered nigh,—but if
Thou lead'st me on to cage, or bar,
Thou wilt shine through my saving star,
And I will kneel where'er *thou* prayest
Away ! I see the storm, and those
My brothers, and *thy* deadly foes
If they could read thy heart, and still
Their blades were sheathed against their will
Whilst thou wert sheltered by this roof
It keeps all treachery aloof.
Away !

HE.

Beloved, and should we fail ?

SHE.

Death will o'ershroud us with his veil
And Love will help the innocent.
Lo, how the breeze uplifts the tent !

I dare not see it long,—its free
Sweet life, our heirloom, Liberty,
Smite like a sword my traitor heart.
But Kismet leads, and I depart :
Fierce Thought is rising from its lair
In my dark spirit, and it rends
Me.   Lead, oh, lead me anywhere
Where Peace and Love can kiss as friends :
Lead thou—I follow thee—and *dare.*

TO SHELLEY.

They call thee less of poet than musician,
Thou whose sweet lays were star-tuned, faint and dim
As morning, when pearl-clouds are in transmission
From Dawn's hands into Day's : and on their brim,
The opal of shed sunsets seems to flutter,
The moonshine of spent summer nights doth lave,
So in each poet-tone thy soul doth utter,
The wing of paling glory seems to wave.
Thou hast no deep fierce sighs that sound like Passion,
When blood is near to foaming ; thou hast nought
That can tempt souls to sin, in mere compassion
Of sympathy with the wild poet-thought.
Thou lark ! (as beautiful as that which soareth,
Within the heaven of thy verse) thy soul,
Whilst veiled in flesh, its loveliness restoreth
To God who gave it, past its own control.
Thy song is as some dew distilled from starlight,
Drops, which refresh the poet-heart that drinks
Unconsciously, deep in mysterious farlight,
Of a new orb, whose evolution *thinks.*

Thou disembodied Spirit, whose white pinions
Winnow pale light (through spheres Earth dreams not of)
Down to the world, from unexplored dominions,
Where song is Life, and loveliness is Love.
Would that my heart in some faint exhalation,
Might lift thee half the bliss which thine has showered
Upon it, from thy free-born sphere's elation !
As fragrance greets the sun from whence it flowered,
As the dew climbs into the fair white fountain,
As the stem labours upward to the flower,
As mists enwreathe and kiss the star-crowned mountain,
As moments roll into their sea—the hour ! . . .
Forgive the wish ! thou through all Time must ever
Stand out unsolaced ; crowd may smile to crowd,
But *kings* must hold apart, on thrones that sever
Them from the dust, and, poet, the white cloud
Of Poesy keeps *thee* aloof and lonely,
Far from the sounds of Earth ; its praise and blame
Can move thee not at all, and reach thee only
Through that far fragrant atmosphere—thy Fame :
Still would I kiss the spirit which has taught me
How near man climbs to God, all unawares.
And for all the fair beauty it has brought me,
And for the love (which every poet shares)
Of the wide Earth, this chaplet I have wove
For thee (it fades *so* soon) from blossoms born of Love.

FLORENCE, *December* 30, 1881.

CAÏQUE SONG.

THE winds are low and the wave is tame,
As a lion crouched on his massy frame,
  When his lip with blood is sated.
Calm and bright are the stars above,
I have lingered long by thy slumbers, love !
  While thy sails with Sleep were freighted.
      Now break the spray,
      From thy silver prow
      We will float away,
      (I and thou)
  Strangely, blissfully, mated
  From the land with a foam-lit vow !

See the lights from the shore-side flash,
Hark to the sound of the Caïque's clash,
  As the palace step is grated.
The water swirls from my waking oar,
We push our lives from the crowded shore,
  Strangely, blissfully mated !
      Thou'rt fair as some bird
      From the lone sea-cave,

When its wing is stirred,
And its sweet voice heard,
With the music of waters weighted!

My peri of the wave, dost grieve
Istambol's star-girt shores to leave,
Though we outward fly together?
See how the blue wave smiles for us,
And the foam runs free on the Bosphorus,
Light as a wind-swept feather.
Come! the brine and we
Will kiss each other,
In mute sympathy
With one another,
While we laugh to the cloud and the weather.

Come! and the pulse of the sea will beat
With untried song 'neath thy viewless feet,
While I guide thee o'er the waters.
One mind is ours, we tune its mood
To that fellowship in solitude
Which our wandering life has taught us.
This thought is blest,
Twin-souls we are,
And we float or rest,
As the wave and the star,
Fairest of Night's white daughters.

May, 1880.

TO MELANCHOLY.

My heart is as a Ruin, where thou sittest
Keen-eyed, and sombre-hued, thou dismal owl;
While oft on overshadowed wings thou flittest,
About the twilight hours of my soul;
Making the gath'ring darkness (which thou fittest
With evil dreams and shrill weird cries) a night
Of horror.   Grief's loud blasts go sweeping strong
Through Mem'ry-shrouded galleries of my mind,
Awaking echoes which had slumbered long;
And yet I would not have thee hence, the wind
Though loud is lonely—through its mournful song
I need some Presence (though it be a blight
Such as is thine) to tell me that among
The Quick I wander still, as the immortals might.

FLORENCE, *September* 15, 1881.

THE HAUNTED STUDIO.

HE stood 'twixt pedestal and plinth,
A chisel in his hand,
His genius wrought a labyrinth
Of thoughts too vague to understand,
And doubts, that rose on either hand
Of his young spirit, to allure
To paths for Youth too insecure. . . .
His master's was a touch that wrought
On ev'ry stone a living thought,
And gave the gods of old a dower
Of beautiful imperious power,
To save them from the dust and death—
Such might ! he almost gave them breath.
His gall'ry, with its marble throng,
Was one unbroken Epic song,
Through which the unextinguished soul
Of Beauty, like a spirit stole.
His master was a man whose art
Was the pulsation of his heart,
Its very life, and whose high fame
Had fired the city with his name,

To be enshrined in flowers, or strung
'Mid lyrics on a poet's tongue.
He was of men a very king,
Such as in Classic lands still spring,
To show heroic blood lies deep
In soil that *will* not let it sleep.
Huge-minded, noble, with a pride
In his high genius undenied—
A splendid pride, that made him strong,
And mindless of the common throng
That praised or blamed.   One only fault
Was mingled in this spirit-salt,
That made it flavourless and shook
Esteem,—no rival could he brook,
To place a seal of higher gift
On stone, to which *his* hand was lift.

His hand to-day is on a group
Of fair Cassandra and her lover,
Who o'er the prophetess does stoop,
To give her back her pledge ; and over
King Priam's daughter comes a look
Of tender, pitiful, compassion,
Such as no mortal hand could fashion,—
A smile half veiled in marble—white
With fearful passionate delight.
His master left the work awhile,
Just as Cassandra's wistful smile

Broke up, and Guido lingered still
Before it, half against his will.

He feels the genius in him rise,
And kindle in averted eyes,
And thrill the hand which longs to free
That smile to perfect liberty.
He hears it say, " Without that fetter
Of fear, *thou*, Guido, couldst do better !"
The strife is hard, and sharp, and strong :
Oh ! *ye* who hold imprisoned song,
Oh ! *ye* who feel the spirit-strain
Of music pent in every vein,
Say if this strife against a long
Resisted pow'r was great and strong !
He stood and peered around, and saw
No living glance to strengthen awe,
Nought but the smiles of lips that said,
" Rise.   Shake the shackles from the dead
And give thy genius freedom, lad,
Spread out thy pinions and be glad !"
He seized a chisel, heaved a sigh,
And gave a timid stroke or two,
If he could only work and die
In the sweet ecstasy that through
His spirit, like a spirit, flew !
He toiled an hour, the smile was born,
He kist the curling lips and wept

Tears of mad passion, which can scorn
The world, when once is overleapt
The bar that held them deep and fast
Within the fount they burst at last.
He knelt, and almost framed a prayer,
In very ecstasy of gladness,
To the white marble smiling there
So tenderly upon his madness !
He almost raised wild songs for her
So strangely did his spirit stir. . . .
He has forgotten fear, and feels
Nought but the blinding joy that reels
Along his brain ; he has o'erlooked
The Will that ne'er such freedom brooked,
Or, if he 'members, still he casts
It by, and revels while it lasts
This new hilarity of bliss
That once, and nevermore, is his.
He leans his forehead on the stone,
And feels his temples hotly beat
Against its chill.   He kneeleth prone
Before his work.   Oh ! it is sweet
To place our Genius on a throne,
And crown and sceptre it complete,
Although in all the earth, or far,
Or near, *we* its sole subjects are.—
'Twas while he bent in gladness so,
A step—a fearful step—drew nigh.

Rinaldo saw the stone, and slow
A vengeance kindled in his eye ;
And a chill smile his lip, it spoke
"Now, Guido, shalt thou surely die."
Day after day he saw the gift
Of genius, in his pupil lift
Its fiery hand, to claim *his* meed,
And Guido's death had been decreed.
" *Who* placed this blossom of a smile
On sad Cassandra's lips erewhile ?" . . .
The lad was silent as the grave,
He would not speak the word to save,
And abdicate his legacy
Of Genius, even to go free.
" *Thou ? thou ?* " Rinaldo seized a tool
And smote him, clinging to the base
Of the fair Grecian, whose pale face
Smiled on. Beside the sculptor-stool,
The boy sunk weltering in his blood ;
A few words struggled on his mouth,
A few pathetic sighs that *would*
Flutter 'twixt speech, warm as the South
And faltering as womanhood.
He "pardoned Christ-wise "—so he said
"But had he lived, ah ! he had fought
And risen by his innate strength
To Fame—or who knows what ?—at length.
God pardon him if thus he thought !"

And then he sighed—fell straightway dead.
The master was not cruel, cold,
But passionate as all his race,
And when he saw the stricken face
Of that sweet lad, he was not bold !
He knelt and raised it to his knee,
He kist the youthful brow, and vowed
Self-death.   Ah ! it was sad to see
Him to such depth of mis'ry bowed. . . .
They shrived him for it,—God alive !
What will this Southern world *not* shrive
To him who rules by chisel, brush,
Or pen ?—they pardoned overmuch !
For this, as ev'ning falls in rays
Of gold athwart this gallery,
If one stand silently, and gaze
Across it—there—one yet may see,
A youth come gliding from the shade,
A ghostly form, and passing fair,
And pause where stood that group, afraid
To lift his fingers, pale as air.
He fights his yearning for awhile,
Then, with a soft relenting smile,
He works at that invisible
White group, for whose sweet sake he fell.

FLORENCE, *April*, 1881.

SUN AND SEA VOICES.

SUN-SPIRIT.

TAKE me, sweet Spirit, to thy cool deep breast,
    And lay foam-hands
On these red brows, that tingle with the weight
Of burning splendours and the Day's unrest
    Of many lands.
Take the spent fever of my heart, and tend
    These parchèd eyes, that bend
Over thy shaded glances, dim with white
    Sequestered light,
Lit at some moony taper green, subdued
    To a Sea-mood,
And press cool lips upon my lips of fire
    And lend
That undulating pulse, that quickens never
    For shade or sun,
To temper mine, which leaps and riots ever,
And hotter grows, as Day wears high, and higher,
    Sea-born one!

F

I oped the doors of heav'n, and Day stepped out,
      I laid warm kisses where
Blossoms were slumbering in their fragrant nest ;
      And wakened with a shout,
The chrysalis, that fretted in its lair,
Whence benedictions on my pathway prest,
Of fragrance, and of humming.   I undid
From mountain-tops the snow-bolts, and unbound
      Waters that leapt to sound,
As from their frozen limbs, ice-garments slid.
But now, sweet Spirit, I would shade in cloud
The rays, that shot life through the numbèd ground
      From their world-grasping lid. . . .
Thou art vibrating with thine element,
That modulates its tone to suit thine ear,
Thou art all tremulous with ocean bliss !
      Around are sprent
Flakes, like dissolving stars that there and here
      Reel in intense emotion, when thy kiss
Goes circling o'er them, like a widening breath ;
      Take me, and kiss to death,
Sweet Spirit !   I will slumber while the waves
Beat rhythmic measures on the pale sea-floor,
    And swell to anthems, in the echoing caves
    And burst through many a door,
Of Nature's closing, where unwieldy rocks
Are pivots, and sea-lichens o'er the locks

Have twined fantastic many-coloured webs,
Through which the surge translucent flows and ebbs.
Take to thine arms, sweet sprite, the Day-monarch
And light him seawards through the circling dark.

Sea-Spirit.

Thy robes are gathered up into the west,
Thou art unsceptred, and thy limbs are old
With weariness, and I would bid thee rest,
But that the sea is rough, the billows cold,
And surges unattuned to welcome thee.
Thine eyes are growing dim ; thy step, so bold
This morn, now totters deathwise to the sea,
Monarch of Day ! Still, in thy feebleness,
Come if thou wilt; draw strength from ocean
        founts,
And we will twine a tender rosary
Of shells and pearls, subdued to shine between
The amaranthine under-light that mounts
To myriad hues upon the surface sheen,
Wherewith to wile thy titan-weariness.
        And the pale lips of Oceanides,
            Shall sing thee to the seas.
                But on *my* breast
        No alien spirit ever homes itself—
            I am a freeborn elf
    Of winds, and waters, and I wear no form
        Reliable, but fade like tints that spring

On tearful days within a rainbow's wing,
        After the storm.
A touch would shatter me to nothingness,
        And evanescence is my fragile breath,
    I tremble into birth, and tremble back
            To death.
If a wind curl the wave, or the sea-wrack
    Is storm pursued, or if a tempest scourges
To a pale passion the resisting surges,
            Ah ! then I fail,
    And from this radiant brink,
    In a white agony of fear I sink,
            And draw a briny veil,
    Which Death's untiring fingers weave for me.
    In the dim, shrouded chambers of the sea,
            To die like thee !

Sun-Spirit.

Die to be born ! be buried to uprise,
To-morrow's morn shall see me rule the skies !
To-morrow's morn shall see thy glorious birth,
If now we languish,—for we are not *Earth*
But *Spirit* both, and spirit lives for ever.
        Then let me sever
Thy being with a look ; and let us glide
Together into gloom, sweet Spirit of the tide.

NEREIDS.

The sea is singing, the bells are swinging,
    The foam-bells under the deep,
The earth is enshrouded, the day is o'erclouded,
    And sun-stars fall asleep.
They fall through the waters, whose restlessness slaughters
    Their life, and they sink,
Deeper and brighter, smaller and whiter
    From the brink.
The billows enroll them, the shadows enstole them,
    With dismal robes,
Which the sea-winds have cloven, the sea-clouds have
      woven,
    Betwixt the globes.
Water and fire commingle, expire,
    In frantic throes,
Wreathing and kissing, gasping and hissing,
    For repose.
Triumph ! the brine, at the sky's far line,
    Has fought and won,
And, a mouthful of glory, has swallowed the hoary
    Old Sun !

ECHOES FROM SEA-DEPTHS.

Triumph ! he sinks, and the Ocean drinks,
    With burnished lips, his being ;

His purple blaze falls in pallid rays
　　(Like a moon which the moon is freeing)
Through our silent haunts, where such radiance pants,
　　And strives, and writhes to be free,
Like a wounded snake, which a trail doth make,
　　To the nethermost depths of sea.
His passion frets in our silver nets,
　　And finnèd monsters glide
In and around where his rays are bound,
　　In the meshes of the tide.
Their sheathing scale looms out like mail,
　　In the new light falling through,
When they grope like shades, from rock ambuscades,
　　To bathe in the shifting blue.
Triumph ! the sun sinks down undone,
　　In a tremulous eclipse,
And faintly turns, where the cold sea yearns,
　　The boon for its slakeless lips.

PAN.

PAN was sitting on the marge
Of the undulating stream,
Where the sunbeams wandered faintly,
And the lilies glimmered saintly,
Fashioning his spirit-dream,
Fashioning it broad and large,
Catching tones of music leaping,
In the depths where waves were sleeping;
And the fuller tones sonorous,
Of the winds which, in full chorus,
Rushed to kiss the sedge-grown brink,
Where the god had sat to think.
O'er his satyr-brow inwoven
Were Thought-prints, and both his cloven
Feet, hung listless o'er the brim.
'Twas a merry morn for him!
Sunnily the landscape floated
In the far, while in the near,
On the pulsing atmosphere,
The broad stream of Light was moted,

And the dust that swelled and swum,
With a rhythm slow and dumb,
Helped to birth, with its soft motion,
All the music silent-throated
Which within the god lay dormant,
Like an unappeasèd torment,
Or an unborn storm in Ocean.

He sat and watched the flexile reed,
O'er which the wind played many a prank
Of untaught melody and deed;
He saw it as it rose and sank
With colour-symphonies most rare,
And cried, "By Pan! if music finds
A dwelling for its soul, 'tis here
It lives!"   He from the vagrant winds
Snatched one slim reed, and stripped it bare
Of stream-wove sheath, then to his ear
A moment pressed it, but no sound
Came trembling through the oozing wound.
"Pain begets sweetness," spoke the god,
And gashed the reed with patient ruth
At every joint, then lips and hands
Applied, and thence, in very sooth,
Faint music issued slow, and sweet
As Spring's first kisses when they meet
Above a field of asphodel.

And soon, outstripping all the bands
Which swathed its birth, wild music trod
Out on the pausing air and stream,
As Light treads down a golden beam.

Oh, Pan a merry morning had !
His soul was bursting into life,
With wings of music lightly clad,
How can a spirit but be glad ?
He spoke the tongue of Nature, strewed
The joyous communing of flow'rs,
The lisping accents of the Hours,
And Winds, out from the solitude
Of his deep soul, in speeches rife
With joy ; the very airs drew nigh,
To mingle in his melody.
He claspt the reed, and when the glades
Arcadian wore the evening shades
That lay like dreams athwart them, Pan
Blew merrily, as a god can,
Upon the pipe he deftly wrought,
In twin-rows fitting as they ought,
Looped by a river-stem.   When Night
Drew sable garments round the Light,
He wandered through the forest with
His reed, which was a shapèd myth,
To all the beasts of field and fell.

The lilies shook their moonlit wings,
Dilating on the waves like swans,
Night-born; for the wind's whisperings
Held nothing half so sweet as Pan's.
The lush-grass trembled at his touch,
The aspen branches shook above.
(Oh! Night and Music, ye have much,
So much to make ye kin to Love!)
And the wild cygnet, sailing o'er
The streams, came down through glade and moor,
With curvèd wings and piercing eyes,
In answer to his melodies,
When Dawn revealed the great god Pan,
Piping, as pipes no mortal man.

August, 1881.

DEAR, the nightingales were singing in the gloaming of
 the garden,
When we met ; and when we parted, fell a break within
 their song.
And the silence was so thrilling, that it seemed to ask for
 pardon
To the Night, that grasped and held it, in a shadowed
 hand and strong.

Then *thy* voice grew through the shadows, and the silence,
 stern and solemn,
And my heart was faint with terror, as that question on it
 smote ;
Though the head was proudly raised, and held defiant on
 the column
(Just as though for Pride *thou* cared'st) of the palpitating
 throat.

Thou hadst kist that throat a moment gone, and praised
 its touch, and colour,
Thou hadst gazed full faith through eyes that held a
 memory within.

And my heart for that went wilder, and the breath came
    chill, and fuller,
As that *other* love glanced softly in—a Vision of my sin.

Sin because I should have *told* thee, ere thy life was
    wreckt in loving;
Sin because my heart was given, given, given past recall
Ere we met, and I . . . I let thy passion take its way, and
    move in
The warm cycle of my life, I thought it could but have a
    fall

(When the truth was out) and bruise thee, in a mild and
    tender fashion,
Never piercing through thee thus in anguish lasting, crying,
    deep,
Mine was not the soul of woman that could measure out
    compassion
To the heart that bowed before her, giving her its life to
    keep.

Mine the sin, and mine the sorrow; oh! forgive the want
    of candour
And forget! (Ye nightingales, sing, break this stillness
    which is pain!)
Oh! the very winds have ceased, and those cold, cruel
    stars look blander
Than their wont. Dear friend, forgive me! Wilt thou
    never speak again?

Never say that thou hast pardoned?—by each sigh, and
    memory tender,
Kiss me once in mute compassion ! look me kindly in the
    eyes.
Nightingales sing out ! and smite his silence, with your
    vocal splendour,
For its passion breaks my spirit, through that pitiless
    disguise.

FLORENCE, 1882.

GIOTTINO.

THERE fell through San Lorenzo's dome
A thousand shafts of coloured light,
Born from the aërial hues that home
Themselves in a mosaic bright,
With all the scenes that droop, and swim,
Through lattice gay or fretwork dim. . . .
Upon the southern wall there fell,
A slanting path of gold, and lit,
A scene one may remember well,
From having gazed so long on it,
In every art, and every whim,
That Genius of a long dead Age
Could give to canvas, or to stone,
That thrice-blest woman with her Son
(The Virgin Mary, and the mild
Eyed Saviour, as a little Child)
One might begin a pilgrimage,
And end it at this very shrine,
From Michel' Angïolo, sage
In triple talent, to the fine

Sweet Tintoret, and that divine
Murillo, whose mellifluous brush
Seems dipt in love, it *feels* so much !
A winter's eve in Laurent's fane,
A small child wrestled with his pain,
The rooted pain some few know well,
Keen, wasting, undefinable,
Which Genius carries like a sting,
Deep planted in its soaring wing.
He was not thus to suffer long,
The death of Life was in his face,
And shrunken limbs, and eyes so strong
With Immortality ; their gaze
Pierced through the pallid, suffering dust,
To show how Heaven's radiance must,
Through souls which at its distant gate,
So long in expectation wait.
His little body was a whole
Unshapely thing, and much misformed,
But gaze beneath the brow that warmed
His life, and *there* you met the Soul.
He was not even blithe and free
Of lip and eye as children be,
But seemed as if some fearful weight
Of spirit, in his spirit sate.
He was a painter, and he knew
Before his tongue, each form and hue,

As if he learnt it ere his birth,
To keep him happy whilst on Earth ;
Nor lived he with or thought, or hope,
Save with his glorious Art to cope.
No parents tended him, he was
A waif swept on this stream of Life,
And if (from Sympathy's sweet laws)
One had not stretched across the strife,
To rescue from the pain, and grief,
This poor outcast, and withered leaf
That floated in a strength sublime,
Down the impetuous wave of Time,
The World had lost a spirit such
As it knows little of ; nor much
It seemed to care, this wintry day,
For Giotto and his guardian grey.
The man was rich in sympathy,
But poor as Poverty in pelf,
Whate'er he earned, was given free,
He kept but *loving* for himself,
And nourished it with hope and care,
That it should blossom large and fair,
As any sun-born bough in May.
And those who past him by, could say,
" Lo, how the plant that 'Selmo tends
Has brought him tenfold love and friends." . . .
He loved the boy, because he saw

None other stooped to care for him,
Although, by some instinctive law,
They, through the wizened face and limb,
Read that some strange thing dwelt within
The child, who through the city trod,
With genius of the demi-god,
Although his frame was sick as Sin.

When half the sprightly Tuscan town
Saw how the Art came floating down
Through the boy's fingers, grave they grew,
And searched their glorious painters through,
To find a name to make him glad,
And thus " Giottino " named the lad.
Who, to requite their faith that he
One day should great, and famèd be,
Drew, on their festa mornings oft
A crowd, to see how swift, and soft
Grew, 'neath the lithe hand (free from pain)
The fair creations of his brain.
And often, when within an hour,
He sketched some pagan myth, or power
Upon the walls and stones, and when
Closed round his work the grey-haired men,
With words of sunshine, to requite
His gift, he trampled out the deed,
In fiery pride, as he would say,

G

"Lo, I can build, and sweep away
The work ye prize !"—and out of spite,
He trod the dust in to destroy
The lightest line, in sooth the boy,
Was something of the demon then !
But 'Selmo, like a guardian saint,
Straightway their clemency would plead,
When, filled with horror at such trait
Of malice, they would turn away,
With purses closed, and angry eyes.
(For 'Selmo had to agonize
In that fell conflict for the pelf,
He never yet had asked for *self*),
"See, Signori, his heart is quaint—
Che vuole—'tis a gifted lad,
But when one lives on hope and paint
In sooth, one well may grow as mad !"
And then the smiles and coin would pour
Down in a small but welcome shower.

Giottino was not kind of lip,
Nor knew Anselmo to requite,
For all his deeds of fellowship
And love, and tenderness, aright.
The last was this—the cripple bore
A strange weird fancy in his brain,
That if he could but paint, before

His death, the two in Laurent's fane
He almost would grow well again ;
At least, he then would satisfy
A painful wish, and gladlier die.
So 'Selmo to the high and great,
Had drawn the boy's declining state,
His genius, and the fearful whim,
That was consuming life in him,
And by much patience—many days
Spent at the Civic doors, and praise,
And sacrifice of food, and rest,
He earned at length this strange request.
And with a joyful heart he turned
To Giotto, who such tidings yearned.

Well, on the eve that Giotto learnt
He should fulfil his dream, pourtraying
The aureoled twain whose beauty burnt
His spirit, as he knelt a-praying,
Within Lorenzo's aisle, he felt
The demon swiftly in him melt
A little space, and clung— and wept—
To 'Selmo whose pure love had kept
All the privations, toil, and care,
He day by day for him did share,
From the poor lad, who lived apart
From Earth, a proselyte to Art.

He wept and promised all he could,
Less waywardness of lip and blood,
More thought, and 'Selmo sadly sighed,
Knowing full well that when the tide
Of Joy, and of Remorse should pass
That they would leave him what he was
Before, a wild and wilful sprite,
An heir of Day, born out of Night.

II.

The picture lay full many a span
Up the old walls, and scaffolds grew
'Neath 'Selmo's hands, who worked like man
Can toil who loves—as love so few !
And then Giottino to his throne
Went up, as kings do to their own,
In royalty of pride and place
Which almost lent his step a grace.
Days flew and weeks, he wrought apace,
Death, too, was busy with his tool
Uplifted, on the fragile base
Of the poor life he had to school
Unto his shadows : but the boy
Reckt little of the pangs that half
Devoured his wasting limbs ; a laugh,
Half demon-born, and half of joy,

Broke from his pallid lips, which said
He'd " end the work ere he was dead."
Day after day the labour waxed
So fair, one might have deemed that Death
Lent power to the hand, and taxed
The gift, upon Giottino's breath ;
Which fainter came, as music grew
Rich, wild and lasting 'neath his brush,
Disguised in every radiant hue,
A revelation in each touch,
That seemed to thrill beneath the eyes
Which dimmed in solving the disguise !
The famed and famous of his day,
Came to approve, to praise, and play
On the lad's soul with questions wise,
But his impervious replies
Grew short, and scant, as they were born
From shyness half, and half from scorn.
When One, from out the twain, was painted
The lad waxed very wan and weak,
Life seemed within him to have fainted,
The shades of Death were on his cheek.
And then Anselmo wept, and pled
For a brief respite, but in vain—
" They *must* be wrought ere I am dead
For I shall never paint again !"

When on the Babe his hand was stirred
His heart leapt like a prisoned bird
Against the fever of his throat,
As though it thence would loose its note,
(And when the pulse beats there *to see*
We know the life must soon be free),
Anselmo, with the grief of one
Whose toil and care will soon be done,
Wrought, like a slave with chains endued,
To gain the boy his daily food ;
And when Giottino turned his head
From the coarse homely meal of bread,
His guardian-angel begged, and saved
Each coin, to get him daintier fare ;
Blue grapes, where sunbeams from a lair,
Struck back the bloom they had enslaved ;
And ripe figs (one may buy a store
For two small coins) : but even these,
Lay by Giottino's side at ease,
His days for loving them were o'er !
And 'Selmo, who had forfeited,
For such, his crumb of daily bread,
Kept the wan secret to himself,
And stored the treasures on a shelf,
Lest in the night the boy should wake
With fever, that no wave could slake,

And call for the grape's luscious juice,
Which Love had laid up for his use.
At last the work was well-nigh done,
The Babe was aureoled, and His mother
Smiled holily upon that Son,
Whom she had borne before all other.
And here a shade, and there a touch,
Would leave the picture finished quite;
But Giotto's strength was gone so much,
That he could scarcely hold a brush,
Save by his Will's triumphant might,
Which fought with Death, a conflict grim,
And half had learnt to master him.
But Death came hov'ring round those hands
That quivered, like a snow-swept leaf,
And were *so* strengthless no commands
Could bid them longer hold a sheaf.
He laid his palette on the floor,
His eyes (with weariness grown dim)
Retraced his death-gift o'er, and o'er,
Dilating on each face, and limb,
Whose beauty (when his life was far)
Should shine in Florence like a star.
'Twas at one sunset that he grew
Faint, cold and pallid, and he knew
Death's task (his ghastly task) was done
Which had before his own begun;

And 'Selmo begged to bear him down,
To the good friars, whose prayers could make
More easy (so ran their renown)
The lonely road he had to take.
But nothing would Giottino heed,
He'd "die before the pictured two,"
And, seeing now how great his need
For aid, his friend in terror flew
And prayed the priests the Cross to bear
Aloft, and shrive the dying there.
They looked the old man in the face,
Then sped aloft with solemn pace. . . .
Giottino hardly saw or heard ;
Upon his work his eyes were fixed,
And all in vain the friars stirred
With prayers (and benedictions mixed)
About him, for, with ebbing strength,
He to his picture turned and prayed ;
But the priests' patience ebbed at length,
And, raising up the lad, they said :
"My son, we come with holy aid." . . .
Then, as the lightning cleaves the cloud
With fire, ere yet the thunders loud,
Across their lurid pathway roll,
So flashed the genius from the soul
Of Giotto, to his glance—and speech
Bade them "depart and pray, and preach

Elsewhere, with canting lip, and whim,
His *Art* was Earth, and Heaven, to him!"
The priests with horror gazed, and nurst
A fury in their silent eyes,
If glances dumbly could have curst,
Theirs closed the doors of Paradise
Against the sinner dying fast,
Strange, and rebellious, to the last.
And then they left him, and he turned
His dying words to 'Selmo's ear:
"This gift is thine, for thou hast earned
It, padre; and, though much I fear
That it should pass for foreign gold,
And into distant lands be sold,
Still, for the long, long years in which
Thy love has made my genius rich,
With many deeds like jewels built
Into this life's most rugged stone,
'Tis thine; I give it thee alone,
Do with it even what thou wilt!"...
He died that hour; and when they bore
Him down, the tapers were not lit,
No friars watched his shroud before,
And when they reached the charnel pit,
The only mourner at it bent
Anselmo, faint with grief—and spent....
He left the picture where it stood;

The priests to win it battled strong,
Because the city found, ere long,
That it was very fair and good ;
And some one, deep in lucre-hood,
Had laid his coin in glittering coils,
To lure Anselmo to the toils.
But for that speech the boy had spoke,
Ere death across his whispers broke,
He clutched the picture in his heart,
And *would* not let it hence depart.

The snow was on the Apennines,
And Winter prest with rugged feet
The Flower-city ; through each street,
The winds swept down in icy lines,
They were so strong, and wrought so well,
One almost thought them tangible.
They struck Anselmo to the core,
He could no longer, as before,
Gain the Piazzetta's sun, and rest,
(The full beams smiting on his breast).
In dead Giottino's canvas was,
What might have warmed him oft, and fed,
He would not sell it, though, for bread,
Nor part with it at all, because
The boy's least wishes had been laws,
And then he might have learnt it ! dead—

And so the cold pierced free and strong,
And struck him down to death, ere long.
They found him helpless on the kerb
Of stone, and deemed he slept ; but then
His slumber was so long, the men
Around him, did at length disturb,
And raised the breast-o'erdrooping head.
" Madonna ! but the creature's dead ! "

The town then let its speeches loose,
" The miser ! diamine he might
Have sold the picture for his use,
And now have been in plenty quite."
The Civic Office thronged the church,
And there demanded as their right
The canvas, while the priests averred
'Twas *theirs*—their murmurs were not heard,
Their protests were left in the lurch.
And he who tempted 'Selmo, bore
The prize—by reason of his ore. . . .

But in the realms were Love obtains
Its guerdon, 'Selmo, from the strains
Of angels, learnt what deathless bliss
Awarded is to love like *his !*

FLORENCE, *November*, 1881.

HOURS.

HOURS are the pebbles which Time's hand flings quickly
Into that sea—the Past ; some sink at once,
Some gleam in Love and Faith, and Duty's suns
A moment, ere they dive to gather thickly
Upon the nether shores of Life at last.
But when Time's hand from casting them shall cease,
And when Eternity, with stern white brow,
Shall draw near to him, with " What doest thou ? "
Time will stoop for them through their sepulchre,
And in quick fingers hold out his increase :
Wherefrom Eternity shall pick the fairest
And leave the hours that unreplenished were
In Time's grey palm—whose lips shall straightway stir:
" And what of these ? "
                              " Do with them what thou *darest !* "

February 8, 1882.

THE SPIRIT OF NIGHT.

THE spirit of Night drove out the light
    From the heavens, and her car,
Through the western gold, its flight unrolled,
    Charioteered by a star.
She caught the shrouds, of the Twilight clouds,
    And into her garments twist,
The petals red, which the sun had shed
    When he trod in amethyst.
She kist the bars of the scalèd stars,
    And they burst like mellow flowers,
Which a touch of the sun has just undone,
    In the heart of somnolent bowers.
With faint caresses she smoothed the tresses,
    Pledges of Love and Peace,
That float and quiver, like a diamond river,
    From the brows of Berenice.
She laid a hand, like a spirit-wand,
    On the head of the Greater Bear,
He growled with delight as he sprung to light,
    , From the shadows of his lair.

She sung to the moon a soft low tune,
    Which the silver crescent heard,
And piercing through the aërial blue,
    Blossomèd at her word.
Then weary awhile, with a listless smile,
    And a Light-throbbing breast,
On the tawny bed that Orion spread
    She sank to a transient rest. . . .
Then arose, and trod, with the step of a god,
    The skies from end to end,
Where the Northern Pole, with its great white soul,
Seems over the whole wide earth to roll,
    To where the Plëiads bend.
She bathed her feet in the streamlets fleet,
    And drew them, sleek as silk,
From the bubbling edge where the billow's ledge
    Sprinkles its beads of milk ;
Then sought her rest on the curtained breast,
    Of the heav'ns a little space,
While the winds breathed low, to and fro,
    Fanning her dusky face.
Then each star sailed wan, like a weary swan,
    Down the streams of the whitening sky,
And the moon withdrew, as though she knew
    That the spirit of Day was nigh.
While Night upsmiled, like a sleep-flushed child,
    And stretched her arms to the Dawn ;

Then rose to sweep down the golden Deep
   Of the billowy clouds of Morn.
Thus shadow-coated, she slowly floated
   To the horizon's brink,
And dipt in the sea, where all things that be
   Their tithe of oblivion drink.

FLORENCE, *March*, 1881.

ARIEL.

"A Pardlike spirit, beautiful and swift,
A love in desolation masked."—*Adonais*, xxxii.

THERE was a Poet born, whose spirit kist
The morning-stars, and floated down as mist,
In this world's shadowed pageant to assist.

He knew no language save the speech that wrought
Within him, like a fine and changeful thought,
(Men deemed he knew much less than mortals ought),

But in *his* tongue he spake all lovely things,
And words dilated as on viewless wings,
Soul-breezes fluttered through his whisperings.

He poured the song into the Skylark's throat,
He set the Cloud in motion, like a boat,
Across the skies of Song, thereon to float.

He had of Earth no knowledge—but his lore
Was wide, for it was learnt his birth before,
And it spread 'twixt the Past's and Future's shore.

He was a radiant spirit—like a white
Star, grown to loveliness on unborn Light;
Yet in his guilelessness there was a might

Which was to guile, and sin, as antidote.
And, with a pow'r which ever seemed remote,
He struck at Wrong, and at Oppression smote;

And tried to clear from off Earth's eyes the film;
And strove of Right's frail craft to guide the helm;
And drove his soul at Evil—to o'erwhelm.

He sung of all fair things, and wept soul-tears,
Because life knew so little of those spheres,
Where Truth is loved and Wrong is set with fears.

He was God-born, although the path he trod
On Earth gave 'neath his foot, and, through that sod,
He struck at man, and dreamt he smote at God.

But his pure spirit set men's laws aside,
(God has no law save Love), and it defied
Their will in calm integrity of pride.

For this, man set upon him the curst seal
Of Atheist—and righteous hearts did steel
Themselves against him.   Heaven will reveal

H

If he who sings, as sang the morning-stars,
God's glory (praising Nature's) truly mars
His birthright, drawing on himself the bars

Of heavenly mercy—or if the new Earth,
Which gave his glorious poet-tongue its birth,
Will stand and judge *him* for *man's* little worth.

God is the Arbiter—He will award
The poet-spirit a supreme reward ;
For God (unlike just man) is never hard.

He reads aright 'twixt sin, and deadly hate
Of all oppression.   Many stand and wait
Through life, with folded palms at Heaven's gate;

But some shall enter there we dreamt not of,
And my sweet singer, being judged above,
Shall enter too—because his life was *love*.

FLORENCE, *December* 30, 1881.

LAST WORDS.

LOVE ! kiss me with passionate lips; we must part at the
    fall of the sun,
When the dews from the Twilight-eclipse, to the ends of
    the firmament run,
When the stars gather holy, and palely, and love seems
    too soft to be told,
In the gloaming's sweet silvery silence, grown out of the
    heart of the gold.

We must part, Fate decrees it, though fearful this break
    in the chords of our bliss,
And a woman's eyes need be as tearful as those that are
    held to thy kiss,
When the strength of her love has up-flowered, to the
    bloom, of the blossom and fruit,
And Life's hand points out to her, dumbly, that there is a
    worm at the root.

The worm of their pride, and my duty, which bids me,
    which bids me forsake,
And Fate clamours over the booty she smites at my spirit
    to take,

And hearts are left blasted for ever, because they have
    learnt over soon,
That spirit is born unto spirit—and that fragrance lies
    latent for June.

Forgive me, beloved ! add not coldness—as if *mine* were
    the finger of Fate.
I lacked not to love thee with boldness—wilt *thou* have
    the courage to hate ?
I have met much reproach at thy glances, but now
    (while thou still hast the power)
Be unto me all I would have thee (just once), for this
    terrible hour.

The birds have all floated and twittered, to rest in their
    murmuring leaves,
The owls are awake, and have flittered away from their
    home in the eaves.
The stars are impassioned with beauty, but chill is their
    look, as the kiss
Which thou givest me here for the latest. Oh ! love, *have
I merited this ?*

I have striven with Life, and been worsted, and at last I
    am bruised to the rod.
I have pled to pale Grief, that in her stead, I might see
    but the finger of God.

And now, when my vision is clearer (though love has not
  suffered for Light
Brought to it by Duty) I've chosen (God help me) the
  love of the Right.

Then bid me farewell but with passion—some warmth
  from thy spirit must slip.
At the touch of my soul, magnet-fashion, and thence over-
  flow at the lip.
Let us feel that the bliss (which is over), the grief, and
  the animate pain,
Have not through our lives been wide scattered, as use-
  less and castaway grain.

Let us feel that when Time shall draw to us, and point
  us the edge of his scythe,
The deep love which now palpitates through us shall be
  tendered unto him as tithe,
And that when his old hands shall ensheaf us, among all
  the harvesting done,
That our lives, now so fatally dual, shall be stilly up-
  gathered as *one.*

December 12, 1881.

ALPHĒUS TO ARETHUSA.

THERE is no wave,
That can hide or save thee,
From Delos to th' Ortygian cave.
And no sea-buds blow,
Like dissolving snow,
Where the might of my love may not reach and
enslave thee.

Thy form is fair,
And thine eyes are milder
Than stars that gaze through the Night's dark hair.
And the touch of the dawn
On thy cheek is born,
And thy course than the roe's wild flight is wilder.

The waves may beat,
And aid thine endeavour,
But after thee rush my viewless feet!
As a liquid wind,
Which leaves Time behind,
And leaps to enfold thee for e'er and ever.

My lips I have sunk
In the weltering brine,
And deep through the Ocean's draughts have drunk;
Seeking those lips,
Through that green eclipse,
That shall yet be held as a gift to mine!

I can see thee go,
With thy wave-lit foot,
And thy flashing limbs like the drifting snow.
Eyes gazing round,
Like an open wound,
To see me gaining in swift pursuit.

I have reached thy mouth,
Which is sweet with laughter,
(And tears dropt through to allay Love's drouth);
I have claspt thy chilly
White hand, like a lily.
Oh! the hours of bliss that come thronging after!

When, close on thy bosom,
I sleep in the sun,
And thou murmurest on like a water-blossom,
Which winds strew thickly
With odours quickly,
And snatch faint kisses from, one by one.

Where the dragon-flies,
Shall above thee wing,
And yearn for a smile from thy dark deep eyes,
Diaphanous pinions
Shall be thy minions,
Yet steal from *thy* beauty the tints they bring.

And the ocean shell,
Like a surge-shaped petal,
Shall cool, and unwith'ring within thee dwell.
While Light at thy marges
In green rings enlarges,
And floats to thy calm depths therein to settle.

The shy-hoofed Satyrs,
Shall stretch and shall leap
At their shadows, falling through thy white waters.
The timid Fauni,
With glances tawny,
Shall stretch at thy brink in a wakeful sleep.

While their leader, Pan,
Shall drink at thy mouth,
Great liquid kisses grown twilight-wan ;
And deem them better
Than those that did fetter,
At Ladon his breath, when the hours were South.

Oh ! fairest of daughters,
Oh ! love of the stream,
Thou white-limbèd nymph of the wandering waters.
All tender emotion,
I sweep through the Ocean,
And clasp thee at last, like a wing-fettered dream.

FLORENCE, *November*, 1881.

INDIAN LULLABY.

Sleep on ! my heart, and through deep Slumber's nest,
Light be the wings of dreams within thy breast,
Sleep in soft bliss—I watch above thy rest,
  As a still star.

Moonshine is floating down, the shivering palms
Stretch o'er the Tank their lithe and shadowy arms,
And all the wind with champak fragrance warms,
  Near and afar.

Lo ! on the brink the snake its white coils opes,
And sends them o'er, like soft and silver ropes,
Some hidden prey beneath the wave he hopes,
  Sleep *thou* unharmed !

All the white air vibrates beneath the cry
Of the sly gheethur * wandering weirdly nigh
As now it swells tumultuously, to die
  Distance-calmed.

   * Jackal.

Sleep ! thy closed lips are like the folded bud
Of the Anar * which bursts to mellow blood,
When the warm day has reached its zenith-hood,
  Love of my heart !

I will ward off all evil things that creep
Near to thy rest ; and shed above thy sleep
Tears, such as eyes that love alone can weep,
  Loved as thou art.

When the large stars look down with eyes of dew,
And the white Dawn comes slowly floating through,
Thou shalt awake, and smile, and love anew
  From thy deep sleep.

Till then dream on ! the jungle tiger's roar
Ebbs like a swell that dies along the shore,
When all its might and majesty are o'er
  On the Deep.

I will avert his stealthy tread and fast,
Thy happy sleep his wand'rings shall outlast,
Nor must thou wake till perils all are past,
  And afar !

Sleep on ! my heart, and through soft slumber's nest,
Light be the wings of dreams within thy breast !
Sleep in pure bliss, while I above thy rest,
  Outwatch each star.

BANGALORE, MYSORE.

Pomegranate.

SHADOWS AND LIGHT IN THE UFFIZI.

In the Gallery's mystic chillness,
    Phantom-forms creep, here and there,
Noiselessly along the stillness,
    Which is rarified to air.
Till our Fancy, down the Ages,
    Pushes mortal barks afloat
On the stream of Time, that rages
    Dumbly 'neath each winging boat. . . .
With his boyish head low-drooping
    Till one scarce his smile can tell,
For the shadows overstooping,
    Comes God-gifted Raphael.
Pondering in his spirit, sounding
    All the lone depths of his soul,
For that smile—our mind confounding—
    Which about the Virgin stole.
There is something sad and thoughtful
    In his side-glance, that prepares

For the pictures which he wrought full
  Of his genius—unawares.
Next him comes a shadow burly,
  With strange features muscle-firm,
And a gaze 'neath brows so surly,
  That one scarce can read the germ
Of the " Morning " he created,
  Close upon the robes of " Night,"
When his spirit lay full sated,
  At the portals of its might !
And da' Vinci, with the splendour
  Of bright fame upon that brow,
Whence the eyes shoot Passion's tender
  Arrows, from a silver bow.
Then adown the shadows winging,
  With the gold of heaven besprent,
Giotto, with his large eyes singing
  Of the glory in him pent.
Rays he cast in ambient beauty,
  O'er the pictures of that heart
Which escaped from Life to Duty
  In the Sanctuary of Art.
And a grave slow step comes later
  Up the dim Uffizj shade,
Hand in hand with that Joy-hater
  Time, who lay in ambuscade

For the form his fingers weighted·
　With the links of years and fame,
He whom Venus once elated
　With the music of her name.

Oh ! dead Painters, with the power
　Of Creation, lying deep
In your souls, shall it upflower
　Nevermore from Death's dim sleep?
Have the shadows chilled your God-gift?
　Are ye smiling on your biers
So content, that were the sod lift
　We should lose the sound of tears?
Oh ! ye Painters, with the vision
　Of heaven's glory, smiting down
In such wonderful fruition,
　Through your Genius' starry crown,
Are ye willing to lie idle,
　With the meaner dust around,
And your aspirations bridle
　To that silence underground?
Did your Artist-spirits linger
　O'er your graves to see Life drop,
Till Grief almost lift her finger
　For the hungry worms to stop?
Ye who painted flesh, that's living
　Through long centuries, as fair

As the day ye left off striving
   With the latest dimple there,
Could ye not preserve *your* features,
   And the happy coming breath
That sent life on, glorious creatures
    That sent life on unto ?—Death . . .
Comes no answer ? Silence clambers
   Up the roofs, and seems to cry,
Through the wide deserted chambers,
   "Who so powerful as I ! "
And the forms of Artists vanish,
   Like a blade-sweep in the air,
Where Fact's Angel stands to banish
   Fancy from Thought-portals there.
But as down the steps we wander,
   Turning back our spirit-ears,
For the words which we would ponder ;
   Through our disappointment's tears,
Comes a vision of pale phantoms,
   Robed in Light, and chaunting low,
And across their soft-told anthems,
   Waving gently to and fro,
We can hear those lips replying,
   Through Time's unremembered dust
(Just as though they knew not dying),
   " We have given back our trust

Unto God, we held by Duty,
   In the talents He consigned
To us, painting forth all Beauty,
   As the reflex of His mind.
And He scatters tenfold blessing
   On us for the labour done.'

Friend into the Piazza pressing,
   Let us go and meet the sun.

FLORENCE.

WITCH SONG.

EARTH'S bosom lies bare
To the kiss of the Moon,
While Night in despair
Drags her softly and soon,
By the darkness of tresses,
To undreamt caresses,
But in his right hand shines a blade, shines a blade !
He will lunge it, and plunge it
Deep down through her beauty the slumbering maid.
We will follow, will follow
Through bracken and hollow,
And kiss the dust shadows which fall from his feet,
And the blood which Earth's bosom shall run with so
fleet,
And the pale sighs she utters,
As life ebbs and flutters
From her Light-smitten lips, when the wound gapeth
sweet.
Shade strikes at the Moon,
To hold Earth and have her,

I

The Moon smites at shadow
. To lave her, and save her,
And the spheres tremble down in a visionless swoon.
Come, sisters, and wing it
While the owls and bats sing it,
We'll scour Night after, o'er ocean and meadow.

First Witch.

As far as that mountain
Which spits through the dusk
A fiery live fountain
Whose boulders now scorchèd once gleamed like the
tusk
Of a boar brought to quarter
A moment ere slaughter.
Come, sisters ! the Evening walks laden with musk.

Second Witch.

Where I saw in the hell-broth,
Full many a soul
Of the lost, going round in a ring as by troth
Their woes they did carry,
To mingle and marry
With the pain they should meet ; and the finger of one
Pointed up to us three, pointed up like a sun
When its fire has burst through all spheric control.

Ha ! ha ! if he might
Have smote to our height,
We three had been charred by his wrath and undone !

SPIRIT OF DARKNESS. *passing in the wind.*

Is it thus ye commune of your master, ye hags?
He *will* reach ye, and seize ye, and tear ye to rags
In your insolent mirth ;
From the regions of Earth
He will scatter your bones in an hour from this,
Down, down the abyss !   [*passes.*

THIRD WITCH.

And above him a comet
Shone steady and pale,
Like God's finger, and from it
Hung stars as a veil,
Which Satan struck frowns at from depths of his ire.
But distance did screen it,
And looming between it
And hell s troubled hate, was God's breath like white
fire.

FIRST WITCH.

On, on ! these bats whirl
Like a storm in the air
And their wings as they swirl
Have a sound of despair !

ALL THREE.

How the winds melt away
Past our flight, how the Night
Stalks along in his might
To the weak Earth, his prey

THIRD WITCH.

The Moon gives her up,
And the blade of the stars
Is shining in Night's swarthy hand, we shall sup
On the cries and the scars
Of the world, of the world, as we sit on the cloud.
And the winds shall laugh with us like spirits aloud !
While earth waxeth dim
In each moon-blighted limb,
And Night smiles o'er her—pitiless Night—till she swoons
Down, down to the depth of his hate, of his hate.
Ho ! sisters, methinks that the hour groweth late ?

FIRST WITCH.

'Tis ten by the wings of the shadows which fly.

SECOND WITCH.

'Tis twelve by the pulse of the hours as they die,
And the bat in the ivy with visions communes.

THIRD WITCH.

'Tis one, oh ! our triumph, our triumph is nigh !

An hour later, all the WITCHES *chanting on the brink*
of Ætna.

Ho, fires ! go slowly :
We drop ye juice of bane and moly,
To quench ye up, to scorch and wither,
And lids of a dead man wrest this morning
From eyes that nevermore wake at dawning.
And just one drop from the heart o'erladen
Of a newly-slain and immaculate maiden,
Whom a lover smote at a jealous rumour.
(She was as fair as the maid who hither
Was born of the Earth and Skies.)   Entomb her
Heart's pure blood, and assuage your ires,
Ye wreathing, hissing, unquenchable fires !

What burning for ever, and rioting still
As if ye would burst as the heart from this hill ?
Tangling in fiery eddies, yet keeping
The station from whence ye for ever are leaping
Upwards like hell-hounds to seize us and clasp us,
Red tongues thrust out hotly for food, would ye grasp us.
We who were born out of fires as awful,
To whom brimstone and flames are the elements lawful ?

Ah ! but we laugh at your hellish endeavours :
Leap at our feet, *there* your impotence severs,
Crushed by our glance from your lurid desires
Ye wreathing and curling, unquenchable fires !

　　　　　[*The Spirit of Ætna passes in a cloud.*

FIRST WITCH.

Sisters, what passes
Like some huge phantom of the Night afloat
　　　　On Darkness?—it amasse
Clouds like dumb waves around it.　.

SECOND WITCH.

　　　　　　　Yet it smote
Me with red glances, till my withered brow
Shrunk scorched to fear——

THIRD WITCH.

　　　　　　Let us forth and surround it
And question face to face th' intruder now !

They clasp hands and dance round the Shape singing.

By the Powers of Darkness pressing
　　On the spirit of the Night,
Which stands round us now, confessing
　　One great fellowship of Might,

And the lost souls wandering, haunted
 By our unrelenting Will,
Who art thou, dim form, undaunted
 By our potency to kill?

Stars are rolling in their courses,
 And these hell-fires run their race,
Breathed on by immortal forces
 Standing with them face to face,
But of all on Earth or under,
 Wrapt in mystery unsolved,
None like thee, thou form of thunder,
 Has before us e'er evolved.

Art thou veilèd Storm that treadest,
 Art thou Ocean-wraith, or Wind,
Gathered into shape that threadest?
 Or the disembodied mind
Of some element new dying
 In gigantic throes? Reply!
What, thou darest, unreplying,
 Pass?—then, phantom, writhe and *die!*

 Quick kill it, and seize it,
 With fires appease it,
Cast it down in the pit where life dwindles and shrinks.
 [*The Shape floats down.*

Ha ! the flames how they flick it,
And snatch it, and lick it
With tongues whose red edge seems so liquid, *it drinks !*
Hark ! how the shape rumbles
And vanishes, crumbles.
Perchance 'tis the demon of Night we have slain ?
Lo ! the heavens are flying,
And melting and dying.
Help, help, from this blaze, and this fiery rain !

        [*Eruption of Ætna with loud thunderings,
during which the* WITCHES *disappear.*

FLORENCE, 1882.

Ἀφροδίτη Ἄρει.

THE spear has deep-wounded me, brother!
And my eyes are grown dim with the pain.
(Thy chariot, thy chariot of fire! to bear to Olympus
afar),
Iris is leading me gently, her robes are the dews of a star,
Which have fallen, a midnight rain.
Thou in this hour canst save, as can aid me (the wounded)
none other.

Ah! fierce were the darts of the Greeks,
My son was in danger of dying,—
Could a mother's breast then be impassive? could a
mother's heart beat unafraid?
Forwards I flew at the conquering, lending my love *him*
to aid
Who was sore prest, yet un-flying.
Brave with the old courage of Trojans—oh! save me, a
sister now speaks!

Thy car and thy horses of fire
To wing me to safety and bliss !
The wound of the mortal is burning like Pain on th'
Immortal's white palm.
I lean on thee only, who bear'st the war-darts aloft on
thine arm,
Thou wilt not forsake me in this
Time of my need, thou Destructor, the terror of gods and
desire.

See my hand shedding blood like the rain,
And the strength glides away from my heart
Of woman, and oozes beside it (brother, brother, thy
chariot of speed !).
The war-din sounds far and disperst (my spirit too faint
is to heed):
War-mighty, oh ! take *thou* my part,
And waft me to safety above ; shall a sister beseech thee
in vain ?

FLORENCE, *December*, 1881.

AIR SONG.

Away! away,
To the lips of Day,
Which are striking chill at the gates of Morn,
For the dewy airs,
That the Night prepares,
In her deep dark breast, for her babe the Dawn.
Dawn comes to life,
Through a transient strife,
And clasps weak hands round its dusky nurse,
Whose shadowy breast
Sinks back to rest,
When new life is drawn for the Universe.

We spread our wings,
O'er the bubbling springs
Of dews, Light-born, which to pure mists curl,
And we chase the dreams,
From the sky's swift streams,
That sweep in invisible tides of pearl.
O'er the tracks which Light
Unweaves to our sight,
As we tread soft measures towards the sun,

And kiss the storms
(That his waking warms)
Of heat, which through night in his loom he spun.

Day laughs to us,
In diaphanous
Sweet smiles, that we wreathe to a freshening gale
For the weary eyes
Of the Earth as she lies
Helpless, in Summer's long arms and pale.
We touch the dews,
And therein infuse,
The breath which we won from the lips of heaven,
When we sailed in might,
To the springs of Light,
And smote at the skies for the answer given.

We are the sails
Of the gathering gales,
And float them through the seas of Space,
Our pennons waving,
Like blue mists laving
The billows, we tread in our boundless race.
And when that Ocean
Is all in motion,
We snatch deep tones from its ruffled lips,
As each cloud, like a vessel,
Sails up to wrestle,
And *we* propel all these phantom ships.

Then Earth gathers round her
These barks that founder,
And tethers each hull, as it driftingly drops,
To anchor slowly
In the harbours holy,
Which the storms have scooped in the mountain tops.

Come ! fairest sisters,
White-eyed ministers,
Ye wandering airs of the central heaven,
And pour your laughter,
The sunshine after,
To temper the unborn storms, and leaven,
With pure white blisses
Of mellowing kisses,
The winds, which Earth's hands have heapèd brown
With Life's leaves, battered
By Grief and scattered
Upon ye, in witherèd fragments down.
Come, wings of Dawning,
Snow-tipt by Morning,
And sweep o'er the wide world's sorrowing face
Through portals (swinging
Wide-open) winging
Our happy flight o'er the tides of Space.

FLORENCE, 1881.

THOUGHTS.

THOUGHTS are the pearls, deep in our spirit's waters,
We dive for, holding in warm Speech's breath,
Sometimes too long, and then we die the death,
Wreckt by the arduous task which (lengthened) slaughters.
Sometimes the sea is clear, and down we fall
And pluck our treasures up with eager fingers,
Heeding the tides of Feeling not at all,
Nor Fancy, that sweet syren, and her singers.
We clutch the spoil, and round the slender throat
Of the fair Hours we string it, sure and fast,
Unmindful that with them it fades at last,
And that dimmed pearls are held of little note.
But be that as it may, we wrestle strong,
For brief is our career—the diver dieth young.

November 8, 1881.

ARAB LOVE SONG.

THE stars have twice upon the desert waned,
The Night-wind breathes its spirit through the trees,
The Simoon's wrath methinks has been unchained,
And stayed *his* steed, whose hoofs were like the breeze.
Ah, woe is me! Ah, woe is me!
I lift the dust,*
For Zarûf must
Return, or I bereaved shall be!

Thrice has the sun upon the bending palms
Unfurled his glory, and the silver well
Lent weary lips its own sweet liquid charms,
Yet greets it not the tinkle of his bell.
Ah, woe is me! Ah, woe is me!
I lift the dust,
For Zarûf must
Return, or I bereaved shall be!

* Alluding to the custom of mourners in the East.

The sunny dates hang golden to the sand,
The cool surei rests empty to the brim,
I cannot stir my weary head, or hand,
Il Allah ! for my soul is sick for him.
      Ah, woe is me ! Ah, woe is me !
          I lift the dust,
            For Zarûf must
      Return, or I bereaved shall be !

He said a gift would at his saddle swing,
When he returned, to meet me in the tent,
But I would have *him* only, if he bring
Nought else beside, as when he turned and went.
      Ah, woe is me ! Ah, woe is me !
          I lift the dust,
            For Zarûf must
      Return, or I bereaved shall be !

Have I not said to every ear that passed,
" Ho, brother, tell me, doth he hasten home ? "
And, hoping ever he would speed at last,
Have seen the shades thrice lengthen ere he come ?
      Ah, woe is me ! Ah, woe is me
          I lift the dust,
            For Zarûf must
      Return, or I bereaved shall be !

Allah Mashallah ! Lo the moonbeam comes
Down to the plain, it brings my soul its bliss,
For there, methinks I see his charger's plumes !
'Tis Samiel, yes, that speed is none but *his!*
   Ah, joy is me ! Ah, joy is me !
    My soul hath felt and feared its worst.
    Forth to the well my step shall be,
   To quench the pain of Zarûf's thirst !

CAIRO.

K

FRIEND, last eve I caught my wayward lips reframing
    that old ballad,
Which we once did sing together, when our hearts beat
    out the time,
In the gloaming's vocal stillness, when the shadows of the
    wall had
Grown to such a rhythmic measure, that one almost *saw*
    the rhyme.
And we two sat gazing Westward, in the curtained, old
    embrasure,
Where the roses in the summer clomb, and lay across
    the sill,
While the stars came thronging softly, like white pinions
    in the azure,
And the bleating from the sheepfold, dropt asleep upon
    the hill.

Do you mind you of that evening? when for the sweet
    first and last time,
We joined hearts, and voices tenderly (before that wak-
    ing fell),

And this ballad caught our thoughts up, stringing them in
    happy pastime,
And I blushed to think how truly, it had learnt *one* mind
    —and well.
But before the words had faded, and before the tune had
    altered,
You did whisper out your spirit, from the fane-light of
    your eyes,
When methinks the measure died awhile (perhaps it only
    faltered,)
As we changed the winging music to the burden of our
    sighs.

Then—when all your vows were out, and when by right
    of intuition,
Which lies deep in woman's breast, I read your nature
    through and through,
Finding there so much of weakness, springing up in full
    fruition,
That I could not find it in me *still* to own my liking true,
Oh ! your passion burst to music ! and in this same vocal
    measure,
Did upbraid me, but I laught to scorn such anger o'er
    and o'er :
And you spoke, " By all these moments, which I gather to
    one treasure
(Just an hour) for my life, you will not sing this ballad
    more ?

"You will keep it safely garnered, in remembrance of this
    hour?
Never waste its magic on the dull and unconnecting
    air?
As *I* shrine it in my spirit, a sweet link, whose tender
    power
Will re-lead me to the witchery of your eyes, and lips,
    and hair."
And I, laughing, vowed assent—the song for *me* had lost
    its sweetness
As the sympathetic magnet tow'rd a soul I deemed *so*
    high;
Just last eve I broke the promise, for my life had found
    completeness,
And I drank the wine of music, through that strain—I
    know not why.

And I would not write to tell you (since all grief should
    be respected,
And a man's heart—be it flesh or fluff—should not be
    trodden low)
Had not Rumour taught me, long ago, how justly I sus-
    pected
That *yours* was not worth the silence you imposed upon
    me so.

And *I*—being conscientious, never breaking heart or
    promise—
Seek release, because that ballad suits my lips so rightly
    now.
And I beg you will consider (what you doubtless gather
    from this)
That I hold myself unbounden by that rash and foolish
    vow.

MARGUERITE

(In the Prison).

THROUGH the darkness—'tis no error,
 I can hear my true love's tone,
And my heart outleaps its terror,
 And goes forth to meet my own !
As a bird hears its mate calling,
 Calling, through the forest storm,
While the thunder-claps are falling,
 While the light leaps live, and warm,
So I hear a whisper growing,
 Through this spirit-storm—so sweet !
And my heart can not help knowing,
 When *he* calls me " Marguerite."

'Tis a long, long name, and rather
 Would I have the first he called me,
For this seems to send me farther,
 Than these walls, where they have walled me.

In the days gone by 'twas "Gretchen"
 Like a ripple in the brook,
He would couple it with " Mädchen,"
 Rhyming it as from a book.

Oh, those days of tender gladness !
 Oh, the lindens and the stream !
Through the pain, and through the madness,
 I can see them like a dream.
Hark ! the winds come through the garden,
 And *his* step, and his sweet talk,
Then the lover's kiss and pardon,
 When we quarreled on the walk !
Sun, and shadows falling dapple,
 Where the young boughs swerved aside,
While the May-blooms, and the apple,
 Quivered down the dimpling tide.

Hark ! he comes, I catch his laughter :
 Shall I climb the grate and watch?
For I hear him coming after,
 Now his hand is on the latch
Of the garden gate, whose hinges
 Creak a welcome shrill, and loud,
Where th' Acacia's drooping fringes
 Cluster down—a silver cloud. . . .
They have put me here a little,
 Just to test my strength—but he,

When he comes, shall snap the brittle
　　Links of my captivity.

They have spread some fearful story,
　　Which is floating in my mind,
Like some phantom shapeless, gory,
　　With a train of fiends behind.
But that mind is turned to madness,
　　And I miss some weighty link ;
I have thought *so* much in sadness,
　　That my brain has ceased to think.
He will come, and lay his fingers
　　Cool, upon my burning brows,
While his tender accent lingers
　　On our unforgotten vows.

Oh ! my Faust, is this not cruel—
　　This long absence ? wouldst thou test
If my heart was ever dual,
　　If it ever loved *thee* best ?
Wouldst thou make our parting longer,
　　Just to have a fonder kiss
When we meet ? Perchance *thou'rt* stronger,
　　But *I* was not formed for this.
Come, beloved ! my fear is calling.
　　Come, beloved ! my sad heart fails.
All the bolts of heaven are falling,
　　All the wide Creation wails

Like a smitten babe.   What is it
   Fills my eyes, my brain, with blood?
Was it some angelic visit
   That sweet dream of motherhood?
Ha! the little hands, they pleaded,
   And they clasped me in the dark,
See, around my neck—unheeded—
   They have left their gory mark!
Nay—'tis but the chain thou gavest,
   Fretting at my throat to kill.

Thou who stoop'st from Heaven and savest
   Save me, *save me* from their will.

FLORENCE, *May*, 1881.

SELECTIONS

(From an Unpublished Indian Poem).

III.

'Twas eve, and its own vestal-spirit shone,
With softened radiance, Gunga's stream upon,
As many an oar, with rippling murmur crept
Along those waves, where restless moonbeams slept,
Like gems all scattered from the sunset clouds,
Grown faint, and pallid, in their billowy shrouds.
It is the Eve when every Hindoo maid,
Who to the river's mighty brink has strayed
(The stream by such reverèd as divine),
Doth to the wave her cherished beam consign.
And, as it flickers tremblingly along,
She lightly cheers its downward course with song.
A thousand lamps are launched the Ganges o'er,
And hark ! a chorus rises from the shore,
A cadence subtle as the Champak's breath,
And yet within it is a wail of death:
While, severed from the rest, Lal Taz entrusts
Two lamplets to the billows, and the gusts,

And thus her care in plaintive song is freed
As wav'ringly they from the brink recede:

" Sail ! sail ! sail !
Till ye reach the billows of foam and brine,
Float and twine !
Twin-eyes from the arching heavens beaming,
In the heart of the daughter of Himarat gleaming,
Shedding your rays as the stars their light,
Wend your flight."

" On, on, on !
Till lost to sight in the river's bend,
Float and wend.
A wreath of myrtle around ye wove,
Wet with the mystical tears of love,
Move, with the pulse of the Gunga move,
Seawards tend !

" One is quenched !
Farewell to love, hope, fear and pain
They are vain.
'Tis a presage true that *one* life has fled,
Swift as the glimmering lamplet sped,
Alas ! for the hour—one Chief is dead.
He lies slain."

There was a pause : and from the sacred shore
Lal Taz arose—her mission there was o'er—

And thoughtfully her homeward way pursued,
To reach the forest's distant solitude,
'Twixt fields, where, watered by the bounteous stream,
The sheaths of Indian cane unfolding gleam,
And gracefully—by evening breezes fanned,
The plumy corn waves o'er the golden land.
With motion light as that which sways the blade,
She onward speeds, her progress not delayed,
By the great lotah * with its welcome drink,
Fresh gurgling from the river's smiling brink,
Which, poised upon her head she homeward bears,
The lightest of her many household cares.
The moon is full, and on her upturned face,
It softly sheds its all ethereal rays,
And half reveals the loveliness which lies,
Safe shrouded, in those melancholy eyes.
Around whose lids the silken lashes creep,
And jealously a dreamy vigil keep.
Her dusky cheek is ruddy as the rind,
In which the anar's † juice is ill confined ;
Her lips are full and flushing as its flowers,
When winds go stealing through their laden bowers ;
And faultless in its lithsome shape each limb,
Which mocks the earth it scarcely deigns to skim,
While silver bells upon her ankles sound,
A cheery march along the dewy ground

* Brass drinking vessel.   † Pomegranate.

Unsought, the fire-flies in the bushes gleam ;
No more she covets the uncertain beam,
Amongst the jasmin in her hair to twine,
Or lay on Shivah's consecrated shrine.

  * * * * *

She nears her hut—and strives (but strives in vain)
To cast aside the shadow of her pain :
She cannot heed the frolics of the kid,
So often fondled, and so seldom chid ;
She does not mark the cobra * silently
Glide to her feet, with dull inquiry,
And subtle motion, for the fav'rite draught
Of milk, which at her hand is daily quaffed.
When once the threshold of her home is spanned,
She crouches where the embers—lately fanned—
Have smouldered into lifelessness again,
Ere she can feel, or realize her pain,—
Ere she can set herself the arduous task,
How to elude her kindred, when they ask
With quick impatience, " if her wingèd light
Had known a speedy and a prosperous flight ? "

  * * * * *

'Tis short suspense—a rush of feet without,
A sudden terror and a thrilling doubt,

---

* Cobras are often kept by the natives as household pets, the fangs
having been previously extracted. They are fed on eggs (which
they swallow whole) and milk.

And woman's voice in wailing o'er her dead,
As swiftly one, into their midst is led,
Pale with emotion, and the recent strife,
The pressing combat, and the hardwon life,
His hair all tangled, and besmeared with blood,
An envoy from the distant camp he stood,
With the dread tidings he was sent to tell,
How in the field brave Shah-Jehani fell.
His mien is fiery and his speech is brief,
With all that sternness which surrounds a Chief,
And ill he brooks their many signs of grief;
Nor stays, his turban's heavy fold to loose,
Nor taste the proffered betel's * ruddy juice,—
He must return.   A sorely needed draught
Of water from the lotah fiercely quaffed.
A benediction on Gangoutri † flung,
And to his foaming charger he has sprung.

    *   *   *   *   *

IV.

'Tis night, and where the jungles near and far
Extend, there gleams no solitary star ;
The clouds have gathered round the pallid moon,
And the still air foretells a tempest soon,
Yet undismayed each hungry beast has crept,
From the dark lair, where grudgingly he slept

* A nut which the natives always chew, and which stains their lips a bright red colour.
† A snowy peak from whence flows the Ganges.

In drowsy watchfulness through Day's hot hours,
Till he (with Night) could reassert his powers. . . .
The tiger wakes—and with a fearful roar,
That scatters terror all the jungle o'er,
Impatiently each glossy limb he shakes,
And through the grass his lordly passage takes,
Secure no humbler beast obstructs his path,
To wrest his prey, or to defy his wrath.
The fierce hyena whose loud yell replies
To the sly gheethur's quick inquiries,
Comes prowling round, to seize the scant remains
Left by the sated monarch of the plains.
Content to tarry till that royal jaw
Rejects some morsel for his meaner maw.
Around, the trees convulsively embrace.
Their gnarlèd roots, a fitting resting-place
For the great serpents, which await their spoil,
In many a scaly and fantastic coil ;
Each keen eye glitt'ring, and each forkèd tongue
Thrust out remorselessly the boughs among,
Skilled at each dart to check the opal wing
Of some fair insect in its wandering,
And with such dainty whet the appetite,
Till worthier prey their vigils may requite.
Above, the boughs in beauty interlace,
And toss sweet blossoms in each other's face.

V.

Hush ! through the forest dim, and deep,
The midnight whispers faintly creep ;
The champak opens all its flowers,
To consecrate the silent hours.
All, all is still along the shore,
Save the murmur of the plashing water,
Tossing on some restless oar,
The music of Himarat's * daughter ;
And a muffled sound—it comes
From afar, the beat of drums,
And the tone of many a fife,
Waking discord into life.
Where the banyan's leaves are spread,
Fan-like, o'er the cactus' head,
And the palms together rise,
Orient pillars to the skies ;
Where the jasmin's pallid star
Sheds its radiance near and far,
Lo ! a chorus dim and sweet,
With a sound of many feet,
Dusky features faintly gleaming,
Where the torches' rays are streaming,
And a bier, whereon is spread,
Peacefully, the warrior-dead.

* The Himalayas.

Rescued from the distant field,
Where his loyalty was sealed,
Fighting 'gainst the stout Afghan—
'Tis the Chieftain Shah Jehan.

In a free space they set the bier,
On the lone jungle's utmost verge.
Why have they borne the slumberer here,
Far from the Ganges' sacred surge?
Nor raised the pyre upon its shore,
As it has been their wont before,
So that, their duty done, they might,
In silence, o'er its gleaming flight,
Scatter, where the moonlight flashes,
All the consecrated ashes?
Why have they borne the fragrant wood,
To kindle in this solitude;
Or hither brought, with pious toil,
The precious and anointing oil?
Oh! they have hither sped because
They seek to break those righteous laws
Which England, wheresoe'er she reigns,
In her humanity maintains;
Because they here would veil the crime
Endeared by Custom, Faith, and Time,
And trust to Night and Secresy,
To celebrate the dread Suttee. . . .

Swift upon the pyre they lay,
Gently, the unconscious clay,
Richly swathed in many a fold
Of a weighty cloth of gold.
Then the waving grass is brought,
And the rising pile is fraught
With the perfume of the oil,
Poured in many a glitt'ring coil,
For the flames a costly food,
On the fragrant sandal-wood.
Now the Brahmin, with a prayer,
Hands to the chief mourner there,
Solemnly, the holy fire
For the kindling of the pyre.

She paused, and leaning o'er the freighted pile,
Gazed calmly on the warrior's face awhile,
One moment scanned the shadowy eclipse,
Then placed the sacred torch upon his lips;
And, slowly mounting the funereal pyre,
With an unwav'ring hand she laid the fire. . . .
'Tis done! the wreaths of smoke revolve and shoot,
And the blue flames leap up in quick pursuit,
The grass has shrivelled 'neath their close embrace
And now they curl about the dead man's face.
While speedily the perfumed woods ignite,
The mourners' pious labours to requite;

And, as the glowing tongues rise high and higher,
The Brahmins chant around the kindled pyre.
And from the jungle near at hand is heard
The tiger's wrath, at being thus deterred,
Kept by the warning atmosphere at bay,
When he can scent—nay almost *view*—his prey :
And the hyena, as he madly wreaks
In unavailing breath, his hideous shrieks ;
While all the lesser crew of bird, and beast,
Gloat in their fancy o'er the human feast.

CANTO II.

"Row, bhye-logue,* row ! kind rest is won,
The palms are lengthening in the sun,
Soon shall we stretch their shade beneath,
And see the fragrant hookah † wreathe.
While mirth shall crown the starry hour,
Row, bhye-logue, row the bahadhoor ! ‡

"Row, bhye-logue, row ! his word is passed,
To-day, this effort is our last,
And he has offered large bucksheesh,
If yonder Ghaût § we swiftly reach.

---

* Brothers. † Pipe. ‡ Lord, or master.
§ Landing-place on the brink of the river.

And then we feast on dhâl,* and ghee,†
So help our progress Gunga-jee !"

Thus sung the crew in their own native tongue,
As lightly on her course the pinnace swung,
By the blue waters which around her swelled,
And by the oars' redoubled toil propelled
The sun's last rays along the scene were thrown,
With all that life met in the East alone,
A flush of glory radiant, swift, and clear,
Sweeping the crystal of the atmosphere,
And robing Sunset in that purple bloom
Which daylight wrought in Hari's ‡ golden loom.
Along the shore, with ev'ry shade of green,
The tropic foliage beautifies the scene,
The light palmetto in fantastic curves,
On ev'ry breeze with yielding motion swerves ;
The fruitful banane from each sheath unrolls
Its silken leaves, like Nature's ready scrolls.
While here and there, the delicate bamboo
Spreads its lithe arms, as though it sought to woo
All the young beauty of the myriad flowers,
Which droop and trail around, in scented showers.
And, mingling in their train, the Sirkee grasses
Bend gracefully to ev'ry wind that passes

* Pulse.
† Butter of an inferior quality, of which the natives are inordinately
fond.   ‡ The Indian representative of Helios.

Across their plumy tufts, which flush, and gleam,
In rosy light, beneath each parting beam.
And silently along the river's lip,
The devotees pray, meditate, and dip :
Or, each observance and prostration done,
Pour out libations to the sinking sun ;
And ere they homewards turn, one moment squat
To watch the ceaseless movement at the Ghaût. . . .

  *   *   *   *   *

'Tis Dawn, or 'tis the prelude to that hour,
When Nature owns illimitable power,
And Night with scanty grace resigns her sway,
At the approach of open-hearted Day.
As yet there is no gilding streak on high,
To warn the jungle dwellers Light is nigh,
But, with that instinct which supplies the need,
They to their vacant lairs unsated speed.
Above, around, a solemn silence dwells
Save where the breeze in hidden music swells,
Through the tall reeds * which whispering respond,
In minor cadence, to their breathings fond.
And the great stars whose dewy loveliness
Grows dim at Dawn, and pale and lustreless,
From the chill skies fade tenderly away,
Like benedictions waning from the Day.

  * The natives make incisions in these reeds, and leave them
growing, for the wind to murmur and make music in.

As yet no bird has fluttered from its nest,
Unfurled its wings, nor plumed its waking breast,
As yet ; . . . but lo ! the skies in silence break,
Night is dethroned, and Morning is awake !
She opes her amber lattice in the East,
And scatters wide Creation's golden feast,
With all the freshness of her star-won dreams,
Life in her breath, and radiance in her gleams,
Fair insects gemming her Light-woven robe,
As forth she floats, to sway the Eastern globe.
From their blue couch th' Hericules ascend
Their azure throne, and to their rule attend,
While—ere their rays too fervidly descend
On Earth—the jungle hears the sudden tramp
Of heavy footfalls o'er its foliage damp,
And cries of triumph shouted from afar,
And whispers (nearer told) of " Khaberthaar !" *
While through the interlacing boughs advance
Th' unwieldy forms of numerous elephants,
Decked sumptuously with cloths of gold, and red,
Each forward by his Mahaut † bravely led.
Who mends the motion of his heavy plod,
Oft by a sudden and remorseless prod.
While, as they onward press, in ev'ry beam,
The gems upon the howdahs flash, and gleam,

* Beware.   † Driver.

Where many a bahadhoor impatient sits,
And eyes the lithe Shikaree,* as he flits
With practised movement, in a quick pursuit
Of the aroused, and now alarmèd brute,
Whose roar of sullen anger testifies
How near at hand his awful presence lies. . . .
Some moments speed—and then a shout of fear,
A plunge, a rush, a cry of " He is here !"
A sudden tumult, and a baffled spring,
A crash of boughs—the hathees † trumpeting ;
A circle formed, then broken wildly through,
The bagh ‡ escaping from their 'wildered view,
And, ringing all around, the cry—" Pursue !"
Already with a bound the brute has burst
Far from the snare he had disdained at first,
But, undismayed, in wild pursuit they dash,
The prompt Shikarees heading the tumash,§
And, foremost (where each struggling strives to win)
The beast that bravely bears him—Leslie Lynn.

On through the jungle's loneliness,
To reach the royal game they press
Where the yielding bamboo canes,
Crackle as they swiftly pass,
Where the close luxuriant grass
To the howdah's height attains.

* Hunter.   † Elephants.   ‡ Tiger.   § Diversion.

And the Cobra startled near,
Notes the strange approach with fear,
Silently their progress eyes,
Then to denser covert flies.
Soon an open space they reach,
Where, athwart a leafy breach,
Suddenly the bagh they see,
Bearing down triumphantly
On them, as they pause.   A sound
Of stealthy footfalls o'er the ground,
Then . . . a rush—a roar.   A bound
From the foliage deep and dank,
Denser than the ev'ning shade,
Where he veiled his ambuscade,
He has leapt the hathee's flank !

One moment of suspense—a fearful yell,
Where in his hide the grip so fiercely fell,
And the huge beast essays with trunk and jaws
To loose the hold of those envenomed claws.
In vain does Runjheet brandish his light sword,
In vain a volley from the howdah's poured,
The swaying motion of the beast in pain
Annuls all efforts, baffles every strain.
The brave Mahaut who less of danger recks,
Reproves, exhorts, caresses, urges, checks :
His charge o'erwhelmed with fear he cannot school,
Disowns all threats, breaks wholly from his rule.

The game is fierce. Another volley hissed.
Nor unsuccessful. Ah ! it has not missed !
The blood is pouring from some sudden wound,
In angry drops along the swampy ground,
And a wild roar of unaccustomed pain
(Or fear) proclaims it was not aimed in vain.
While with that energy of fell despair,
Which Death inspires, or Agony lays bare,
When ev'ry effort, as the life ebbs fast,
Grows fainter, till the fiercest is the *last*,
So, feeling strength forsake which has upheld
Till now, by that same energy impelled,
The tiger seizes in a fatal bound
The form above, and drags it to the ground !

      *   *   *   *   *

INDIA, 1880.

INDIAN SERENATA.

On the brink of the tank,
 Sit long files of shade,
In the wan grass dank,
 As in ambuscade,
Where the serpent coils
 His venomous toils,
Till the moon shine full on the whitening bank.
 Then these lines grow strong
 With their hideous song,
Which breaks on the air like a wild halloo,
 Voices as grim
 As a dead man's limb :
" Ho, friends, would ye feast on the dead Hindoo ? "
 " Where, where, where ? "
 Gasps on the air,
From that ghastly crew, while their lank sides groan
 With the hunger clawing
 Their vitals, gnawing
The jaws, that would feast on a human bone.

First Jackal.

"Over the plain when the stars came blue,
  I saw the train to the jungle wend,
And the pyre was raised, and the flames burst through
  And licked at the limbs of a human friend.
      But the flame may have sped,
      As a kiss o'er the dead,
  And have left some flesh, for a suffering maw:
      So come, dear brothers,
      And famished mothers,
  And feast at the pyre I sniffed and saw."

Chorus.

" *We* come, to the dead Hindoo,
And bury our fangs in his singèd flesh,
      But didst thou see
      That the flames burst free,
Was there never a limb left smooth and fresh?"

All.

"Dead Hindoo—dead Hindoo!"

The hours speed ere the gloaming homes
Its smile in the night, and those hideous gnomes
(Lips all wet with the blood of man),
Trot to the tank as fleet as they can,

Sit on their half-replenished haunches,
While their leader harangues them thus, and launches
His voice once more on the deadly air,
That floats from the white snake upcoiled there :—

" Friends, did ye feast with a happy will ?
How fair was the graveyard, how sweet and still !
Nothing to hold us aloof through the gloom,
From the fresh turned earth, o'er the white man's tomb.
Little to come 'twixt his bones, and the teeth.
How fresh was the blood ! how the tide did seethe !
The hands were fair, but the head was best,
Never a bite from the coffined breast.
Ha ! but we laboured and tore at the wood,
To strip the coffer and reach the blood,
In sooth our jaws are so rent with the pain,
That methinks they will pause ere the like again."

SECOND GHEETHUR.*

"Thou speakest fair, thou speakest true,
But where is the pyre of the dead Hindoo ?"

FIRST GHEETHUR.

"We will wait for the day."

* Jackal.

CHORUS OF JACKALS.

" No ! the ravenous kite,
Will have swooped to the prey,
And have taken flight."

FIRST GHEETHUR.

" We will wait for the dawn."

CHORUS.

" No ! the leopard comes on the latch of Morn."

FIRST VOICE.

" We will wait an hour."

CHORUS.

" No ! the tiger is a midnight power."

FIRST VOICE.

" Let us rove anew."

CHORUS.

" Away ! away to the dead Hindoo ! "

They grope like a band of evil sprites,
To the jungle's edge, where the pyre lights

Are dying deep to the ashes down,
And never a limb is left to devour;
Here a fragment, and there a bone
Split apart by the furnace' power,
  Strewing the ground alone.

But the frantic yells of the gheethur's flew
Back to the tank where the snake upgrew,
To gaze at the dawn, with the charmer's eye,
To teach all the new-born lives to die
In its fangs, as pitiless as those
Which raked up the dead from their last repose,
   And came this cry
   On the morning air
  " Dead Hindoo—dead Hindoo,—
   Where—where—where?"

CALCUTTA.

PRINTED BY WILLIAM CLOWES AND SONS, LIMITED, LONDON AND BECCLES.

A LIST OF

KEGAN PAUL, TRENCH & CO.'S

PUBLICATIONS.

1, *Paternoster Square,*
London.

A LIST OF
KEGAN PAUL, TRENCH & CO.'S
PUBLICATIONS.

CONTENTS.

GENERAL LITERATURE.

ADAMSON, H. T., B.D.—The Truth as it is in Jesus. Crown 8vo, 8s. 6d.

The Three Sevens. Crown 8vo, 5s. 6d.

The Millennium; or, the Mystery of God Finished. Crown 8vo, 6s.

A. K. H. B.—From a Quiet Place. A New Volume of Sermons. Crown 8vo, 5s.

ALLEN, Rev. R., M.A.—Abraham: his Life, Times, and Travels, 3800 years ago. With Map. Second Edition. Post 8vo, 6s.

ALLIES, T. W., M.A.—Per Crucem ad Lucem. The Result of a Life. 2 vols. Demy 8vo, 25s.

A Life's Decision. Crown 8vo, 7s. 6d.

AMOS, Professor Sheldon.—The History and Principles of the Civil Law of Rome. An aid to the Study of Scientific and Comparative Jurisprudence. Demy 8vo. 16s.

ANDERDON, Rev. W. H.—Fasti Apostolici; a Chronology of the Years between the Ascension of our Lord and the Martyrdom of SS. Peter and Paul. Second Edition. Crown 8vo, 2s. 6d.

Evenings with the Saints. Crown 8vo, 5s.

ARMSTRONG, Richard A., B.A.—Latter-Day Teachers. Six Lectures. Small crown 8vo, 2s. 6d.

AUBERTIN, J. J.—A Flight to Mexico. With Seven full-page Illustrations and a Railway Map of Mexico. Crown 8vo, 7s. 6d.

BADGER, George Percy, D.C.L.—An English–Arabic Lexicon. In which the equivalent for English Words and Idiomatic Sentences are rendered into literary and colloquial Arabic. Royal 4to, £9 9s.

BAGEHOT, Walter.—The English Constitution. Third Edition. Crown 8vo, 7s. 6d.

    Lombard Street. A Description of the Money Market. Eighth Edition. Crown 8vo, 7s. 6d.

    Some Articles on the Depreciation of Silver, and Topics connected with it. Demy 8vo, 5s.

BAGENAL, Philip H.—The American-Irish and their Influence on Irish Politics. Crown 8vo, 5s.

BAGOT, Alan, C.E.—Accidents in Mines: their Causes and Prevention. Crown 8vo, 6s.

    The Principles of Colliery Ventilation. Second Edition, greatly enlarged. Crown 8vo, 5s.

BAKER, Sir Sherston, Bart.—The Laws relating to Quarantine. Crown 8vo, 12s. 6d.

BALDWIN, Capt. J. H.—The Large and Small Game of Bengal and the North-Western Provinces of India. With 18 Illustrations. New and Cheaper Edition. Small 4to, 10s. 6d.

BALLIN, Ada S. and F. L.—A Hebrew Grammar. With Exercises selected from the Bible. Crown 8vo, 7s. 6d.

BARCLAY, Edgar.—Mountain Life in Algeria. With numerous Illustrations by Photogravure. Crown 4to, 16s.

BARLOW, James H.—The Ultimatum of Pessimism. An Ethical Study. Demy 8vo, 6s.

BARNES, William.—Outlines of Redecraft (Logic). With English Wording. Crown 8vo, 3s.

BAUR, Ferdinand, Dr. Ph.—A Philological Introduction to Greek and Latin for Students. Translated and adapted from the German, by C. KEGAN PAUL, M.A., and E. D. STONE, M.A. Third Edition. Crown 8vo, 6s.

BELLARS, Rev. W.—The Testimony of Conscience to the Truth and Divine Origin of the Christian Revelation. Burney Prize Essay. Small crown 8vo, 3s. 6d.

BELLINGHAM, Henry, M.P.—Social Aspects of Catholicism and Protestantism in their Civil Bearing upon Nations. Translated and adapted from the French of M. le BARON DE HAULLEVILLE. With a preface by His Eminence CARDINAL MANNING. Second and Cheaper Edition. Crown 8vo, 3s. 6d.

BELLINGHAM H. Belsches Graham.—**Ups and Downs of Spanish Travel.** Second Edition. Crown 8vo. 5s.

BENN, Alfred W.—**The Greek Philosophers.** 2 vols. Demy 8vo, 28s.

BENT, J. Theodore.—**Genoa:** How the Republic Rose and Fell. With 18 Illustrations. Demy 8vo, 18s.

BLOOMFIELD, The Lady.—**Reminiscences of Court and Diplomatic Life.** New and Cheaper Edition. With Frontispiece. Crown 8vo, 6s.

BLUNT, The Ven. Archdeacon.—**The Divine Patriot, and other Sermons.** Preached in Scarborough and in Cannes. New and Cheaper Edition. Crown 8vo, 4s. 6d.

BLUNT, Wilfred S.—**The Future of Islam.** Crown 8vo, 6s.

BONWICK, J., F.R.G.S.—**Pyramid Facts and Fancies.** Crown 8vo, 5s.

BOUVERIE-PUSEY, S. E. B.—**Permanence and Evolution.** An Inquiry into the Supposed Mutability of Animal Types. Crown 8vo, 5s.

BOWEN, H. C., M.A.—**Studies in English.** For the use of Modern Schools. Third Edition. Small crown 8vo, 1s. 6d.

English Grammar for Beginners. Fcap. 8vo, 1s.

BRADLEY, F. H.—**The Principles of Logic.** Demy 8vo, 16s.

BRIDGETT, Rev. T. E.—**History of the Holy Eucharist in Great Britain.** 2 vols. Demy 8vo, 18s.

BRODRICK, the Hon. G. C.—**Political Studies.** Demy 8vo, 14s.

BROOKE, Rev. S. A.—**Life and Letters of the Late Rev. F. W. Robertson, M.A.** Edited by.

    I. Uniform with Robertson's Sermons. **2 vols.** With Steel Portrait. 7s. 6d.
    II. Library Edition. With Portrait. 8vo, 12s.
    III. A Popular Edition. In 1 vol., 8vo, 6s.

The Fight of Faith. Sermons preached on various occasions. Fifth Edition. Crown 8vo, 7s. 6d.

The Spirit of the Christian Life. New and Cheaper Edition. Crown 8vo, 5s.

Theology in the English Poets.— Cowper, Coleridge, Wordsworth, and Burns. Fifth and Cheaper Edition. Post 8vo, 5s.

Christ in Modern Life. Sixteenth and Cheaper Edition. Crown 8vo, 5s.

Sermons. First Series. Thirteenth and Cheaper Edition. Crown 8vo, 5s.

Sermons. Second Series. Sixth and Cheaper Edition. Crown 8vo, 5s.

BROWN, Rev. J. Baldwin, B.A.—**The Higher Life.** Its Reality, Experience, and Destiny. Fifth Edition. Crown 8vo, 5s.

Doctrine of Annihilation in the Light of the Gospel of Love. Five Discourses. Fourth Edition. Crown 8vo, 2s. 6d.

The Christian Policy of Life. A Book for Young Men of Business. Third Edition. Crown 8vo, 3s. 6d.

BROWN, S. Borton, B.A.—**The Fire Baptism of all Flesh;** or, the Coming Spiritual Crisis of the Dispensation. Crown 8vo, 6s.

BROWNBILL, John.—**Principles of English Canon Law.** Part I. General Introduction. Crown 8vo, 6s.

BROWNE, W. R.—**The Inspiration of the New Testament.** With a Preface by the Rev. J. P. NORRIS, D.D. Fcap. 8vo, 2s. 6d.

BURTON, Mrs. Richard.—**The Inner Life of Syria, Palestine, and the Holy Land.** Cheaper Edition in one volume. Large post 8vo. 7s. 6d.

BUSBECQ, Ogier Ghiselin de.—**His Life and Letters.** By CHARLES THORNTON FORSTER, M.A., and F. H. BLACKBURNE DANIELL, M.A. 2 vols. With Frontispieces. Demy 8vo, 24s.

CARPENTER, W. B., LL.D., M.D., F.R.S., etc.—**The Principles of Mental Physiology.** With their Applications to the Training and Discipline of the Mind, and the Study of its Morbid Conditions. Illustrated. Sixth Edition. 8vo, 12s.

CERVANTES.—**The Ingenious Knight Don Quixote de la Mancha.** A New Translation from the Originals of 1605 and 1608. By A. J. DUFFIELD. With Notes. 3 vols. Demy 8vo, 42s.

Journey to Parnassus. Spanish Text, with Translation into English Tercets, Preface, and Illustrative Notes, by JAMES Y. GIBSON. Crown 8vo, 12s.

CHEYNE, Rev. T. K.—**The Prophecies of Isaiah.** Translated with Critical Notes and Dissertations. 2 vols. Second Edition. Demy 8vo, 25s.

CLAIRAUT.—**Elements of Geometry.** Translated by Dr. KAINES. With 145 Figures. Crown 8vo, 4s. 6d.

CLAYDEN, P. W.—**England under Lord Beaconsfield.** The Political History of the Last Six Years, from the end of 1873 to the beginning of 1880. Second Edition, with Index and continuation to March, 1880. Demy 8vo, 16s.

Samuel Sharpe. Egyptologist and Translator of the Bible. Crown 8vo, 6s.

CLIFFORD, Samuel.—**What Think Ye of Christ?** Crown 8vo. 6s.

CLODD, Edward, F.R.A.S.—**The Childhood of the World:** a Simple Account of Man in Early Times. Seventh Edition. Crown 8vo, 3s.

A Special Edition for Schools. 1s.

CLODD, Edward, F.R.A.S.—continued.

The Childhood of Religions. Including a Simple Account of the Birth and Growth of Myths and Legends. Eighth Thousand. Crown 8vo, 5*s*.
A Special Edition for Schools. 1*s*. 6*d*.

Jesus of Nazareth. With a brief sketch of Jewish History to the Time of His Birth. Small crown 8vo, 6*s*.

COGHLAN, J. Cole, D.D.—**The Modern Pharisee and other Sermons.** Edited by the Very Rev. H. H. DICKINSON, D.D., Dean of Chapel Royal, Dublin. New and Cheaper Edition. Crown 8vo, 7*s*. 6*d*.

COLERIDGE, Sara.—**Memoir and Letters of Sara Coleridge.** Edited by her Daughter. With Index. Cheap Edition. With Portrait. 7*s*. 6*d*.

Collects Exemplified. Being Illustrations from the Old and New Testaments of the Collects for the Sundays after Trinity. By the Author of "A Commentary on the Epistles and Gospels." Edited by the Rev. JOSEPH JACKSON. Crown 8vo, 5*s*.

CONNELL, A. K.—**Discontent and Danger in India.** Small crown 8vo, 3*s*. 6*d*.

The Economic Revolution of India. Crown 8vo, 5*s*.

CORY, William.—**A Guide to Modern English History.** Part I. —MDCCCXV.-MDCCCXXX. Demy 8vo, 9*s*. Part II.— MDCCCXXX.-MDCCCXXXV., 15*s*.

COTTERILL, H. B.—**An Introduction to the Study of Poetry.** Crown 8vo, 7*s*. 6*d*.

COX, Rev. Sir George W., M.A., Bart.—**A History of Greece from the Earliest Period to the end of the Persian War.** New Edition. 2 vols. Demy 8vo, 36*s*.

The Mythology of the Aryan Nations. New Edition. Demy 8vo, 16*s*.

Tales of Ancient Greece. New Edition. Small crown 8vo, 6*s*.

A Manual of Mythology in the form of Question and Answer. New Edition. Fcap. 8vo, 3*s*.

An Introduction to the Science of Comparative Mythology and Folk-Lore. Second Edition. Crown 8vo. 7*s*. 6*d*.

COX, Rev. Sir G. W., M.A., Bart., and JONES, Eustace Hinton.— **Popular Romances of the Middle Ages.** Second Edition, in 1 vol. Crown 8vo, 6*s*.

COX, Rev. Samuel, D.D.—**Salvator Mundi ;** or, Is Christ the Saviour of all Men? Eighth Edition. Crown 8vo, 5*s*.

The Genesis of Evil, and other Sermons, mainly expository. Third Edition. Crown 8vo, 6*s*.

COX, *Rev. Samuel, D.D.—continued.*

> **A Commentary on the Book of Job.** With a Translation. Demy 8vo, 15*s.*

> **The Larger Hope.** A Sequel to "Salvator Mundi." 16mo, 1*s.*

CRAVEN, *Mrs.*—**A Year's Meditations.** Crown 8vo, 6*s.*

CRAWFURD, *Oswald.*—**Portugal, Old and New.** With Illustrations and Maps. New and Cheaper Edition. Crown 8vo, 6*s.*

CROZIER, *John Beattie, M.B.*—**The Religion of the Future.** Crown 8vo, 6*s.*

Cyclopædia of Common Things. Edited by the Rev. Sir GEORGE W. Cox, Bart., M.A. With 500 Illustrations. Third Edition. Large post 8vo, 7*s.* 6*d.*

DAVIDSON, *Rev. Samuel, D.D., LL.D.*—**Canon of the Bible:** Its Formation, History, and Fluctuations. Third and Revised Edition. Small crown 8vo, 5*s.*

> **The Doctrine of Last Things** contained in the New Testament compared with the Notions of the Jews and the Statements of Church Creeds. Small crown 8vo, 3*s.* 6*d.*

DAVIDSON, *Thomas.*—**The Parthenon Frieze,** and other Essays. Crown 8vo, 6*s.*

DAWSON, *Geo., M.A.* **Prayers, with a Discourse on Prayer.** Edited by his Wife. Eighth Edition. Crown 8vo, 6*s.*

> **Sermons on Disputed Points and Special Occasions.** Edited by his Wife. Fourth Edition. Crown 8vo, 6*s.*

> **Sermons on Daily Life and Duty.** Edited by his Wife. Fourth Edition. Crown 8vo, 6*s.*

> **The Authentic Gospel.** A New Volume of Sermons. Edited by GEORGE ST. CLAIR. Third Edition. Crown 8vo, 6*s.*

> **Three Books of God: Nature, History, and Scripture.** Sermons edited by GEORGE ST. CLAIR. Crown 8vo, 6*s.*

DE JONCOURT, *Madame Marie.*—**Wholesome Cookery.** Crown 8vo, 3*s.* 6*d.*

DE LONG, *Lieut. Com. G. W.*—**The Voyage of the Jeannette.** The Ship and Ice Journals of. Edited by his Wife, EMMA DE LONG. With Portraits, Maps, and many Illustrations on wood and stone. 2 vols. Demy 8vo. 36*s.*

DESPREZ, *Phillip S., B.D.*—**Daniel and John ;** or, the Apocalypse of the Old and that of the New Testament. Demy 8vo, 12*s.*

DOWDEN, *Edward, LL.D.*—**Shakspere:** a Critical Study of his Mind and Art. Sixth Edition. Post 8vo, 12*s.*

> **Studies in Literature, 1789-1877.** Second and Cheaper Edition. Large post 8vo, 6*s.*

DUFFIELD, A. J.—Don Quixote: his Critics and Commentators. With a brief account of the minor works of MIGUEL DE CERVANTES SAAVEDRA, and a statement of the aim and end of the greatest of them all. A handy book for general readers. Crown 8vo, 3s. 6d.

DU MONCEL, Count.—The Telephone, the Microphone, and the Phonograph. With 74 Illustrations. Second Edition. Small crown 8vo, 5s.

EDGEWORTH, F. Y.—Mathematical Psychics. An Essay on the Application of Mathematics to Social Science. Demy 8vo, 7s. 6d.

Educational Code of the Prussian Nation, in its Present Form. In accordance with the Decisions of the Common Provincial Law, and with those of Recent Legislation. Crown 8vo, 2s. 6d.

Education Library. Edited by PHILIP MAGNUS :—

An Introduction to the History of Educational Theories. By OSCAR BROWNING, M.A. Second Edition. 3s. 6d.

Old Greek Education. By the Rev. Prof. MAHAFFY, M.A. 3s. 6d.

School Management. Including a general view of the work of Education, Organization and Discipline. By JOSEPH LANDON. Second Edition. 6s.

Eighteenth Century Essays. Selected and Edited by AUSTIN DOBSON. With a Miniature Frontispiece by R. Caldecott. Parchment Library Edition, 6s. ; vellum, 7s. 6d.

ELSDALE, Henry.—Studies in Tennyson's Idylls. Crown 8vo, 5s.

ELYOT, Sir Thomas.—The Boke named the Gouernour. Edited from the First Edition of 1531 by HENRY HERBERT STEPHEN CROFT, M.A., Barrister-at-Law. With Portraits of Sir Thomas and Lady Elyot, copied by permission of her Majesty from Holbein's Original Drawings at Windsor Castle. 2 vols. Fcap. 4to, 50s.

Enoch the Prophet. The Book of. Archbishop LAURENCE's Translation, with an Introduction by the Author of "The Evolution of Christianity." Crown 8vo, 5s.

Eranus. A Collection of Exercises in the Alcaic and Sapphic Metres. Edited by F. W. CORNISH, Assistant Master at Eton. Crown 8vo, 2s.

EVANS, Mark.—The Story of Our Father's Love, told to Children. Sixth and Cheaper Edition. With Four Illustrations. Fcap. 8vo, 1s. 6d.

EVANS, Mark—continued.

A Book of Common Prayer and Worship for Household Use, compiled exclusively from the Holy Scriptures. Second Edition. Fcap. 8vo, 1s.

The Gospel of Home Life. Crown 8vo, 4s. 6d.

The King's Story-Book. In Three Parts. Fcap. 8vo, 1s. 6d. each.

*** Parts I. and II. with Eight Illustrations and Two Picture Maps, now ready.

"Fan Kwae" at Canton before Treaty Days 1825-1844. By an old Resident. With Frontispiece. Crown 8vo, 5s.

FLECKER, Rev. Eliezer.—**Scripture Onomatology.** Being Critical Notes on the Septuagint and other versions. Crown 8vo, 3s. 6d.

FLOREDICE, W. H.—**A Month among the Mere Irish.** Small crown 8vo, 5s.

GARDINER, Samuel R., and J. BASS MULLINGER, M.A.—**Introduction to the Study of English History.** Large Crown 8vo, 9s.

GARDNER, Dorsey.—**Quatre Bras, Ligny, and Waterloo.** A Narrative of the Campaign in Belgium, 1815. With Maps and Plans. Demy 8vo, 16s.

Genesis in Advance of Present Science. A Critical Investigation of Chapters I.-IX. By a Septuagenarian Beneficed Presbyter. Demy 8vo. 10s. 6d.

GENNA, E.—**Irresponsible Philanthropists.** Being some Chapters on the Employment of Gentlewomen. Small crown 8vo, 2s. 6d.

GEORGE, Henry.—**Progress and Poverty :** An Inquiry into the Causes of Industrial Depressions, and of Increase of Want with Increase of Wealth. The Remedy. Second Edition. Post 8vo, 7s. 6d. Also a Cheap Edition. Limp cloth, 1s. 6d. Paper covers, 1s.

GIBSON, James Y.—**Journey to Parnassus.** Composed by MIGUEL DE CERVANTES SAAVEDRA. Spanish Text, with Translation into English Tercets, Preface, and Illustrative Notes, by. Crown 8vo, 12s.

Glossary of Terms and Phrases. Edited by the Rev. H. PERCY SMITH and others. Medium 8vo, 12s.

GLOVER, F., M.A.—**Exempla Latina.** A First Construing Book, with Short Notes, Lexicon, and an Introduction to the Analysis of Sentences. Fcap. 8vo, 2s.

GOLDSMID, Sir Francis Henry, Bart., Q.C., M.P.—**Memoir of.** With Portrait. Second Edition, Revised. Crown 8vo, 6s.

GOODENOUGH, *Commodore J. G.*—Memoir of, with Extracts from his Letters and Journals. Edited by his Widow. With Steel Engraved Portrait. Square 8vo, 5*s.*

₊₊* Also a Library Edition with Maps, Woodcuts, and Steel Engraved Portrait. Square post 8vo, 14*s.*

GOSSE, *Edmund W.*—Studies in the Literature of Northern Europe. With a Frontispiece designed and etched by Alma Tadema. New and Cheaper Edition. Large crown 8vo, 6*s.*

Seventeenth Century Studies. A Contribution to the History of English Poetry. Demy 8vo, 10*s.* 6*d.*

GOULD, *Rev. S. Baring, M.A.*—Germany, Present and Past. New and Cheaper Edition. Large crown 8vo, 7*s.* 6*d.*

GOWAN, *Major Walter E.*—A. Ivanoff's Russian Grammar. (16th Edition.) Translated, enlarged, and arranged for use of Students of the Russian Language. Demy 8vo, 6*s.*

GOWER, *Lord Ronald.* My Reminiscences. Second Edition. 2 vols. With Frontispieces. Demy 8vo, 30*s.*

GRAHAM, *William, M.A.*—The Creed of Science, Religious, Moral, and Social. Demy 8vo, 6*s.*

GRIFFITH, *Thomas, A.M.*—The Gospel of the Divine Life: a Study of the Fourth Evangelist. Demy 8vo, 14*s.*

GRIMLEY, *Rev. H. N., M.A.*—Tremadoc Sermons, chiefly on the Spiritual Body, the Unseen World, and the Divine Humanity. Third Edition. Crown 8vo, 6*s.*

HAECKEL, *Prof. Ernst.*—The History of Creation. Translation revised by Professor E. RAY LANKESTER, M.A., F.R.S. With Coloured Plates and Genealogical Trees of the various groups of both Plants and Animals. 2 vols. Third Edition. Post 8vo, 32*s.*

The History of the Evolution of Man. With numerous Illustrations. 2 vols. Post 8vo, 32*s.*

A Visit to Ceylon. Post 8vo, 7*s.* 6*d.*

Freedom in Science and Teaching. With a Prefatory Note by T. H. HUXLEY, F.R.S. Crown 8vo, 5*s.*

HALF-CROWN SERIES :—

A Lost Love. By ANNA C. OGLE [Ashford Owen].

Sister Dora : a Biography. By MARGARET LONSDALE.

True Words for Brave Men : a Book for Soldiers and Sailors. By the late CHARLES KINGSLEY.

An Inland Voyage. By R. L. STEVENSON.

Travels with a Donkey. By R. L. STEVENSON.

HALF-CROWN SERIES—*continued.*

Notes of Travel : being Extracts from the Journals of Count VON MOLTKE.

English Sonnets. Collected and Arranged by J. DENNIS.

London Lyrics. By F. LOCKER.

Home Songs for Quiet Hours. By the Rev. Canon R. H. BAYNES.

HAWEIS, Rev. H. R., M.A.—**Current Coin.** Materialism—The Devil—Crime—Drunkenness—Pauperism—Emotion—Recreation —The Sabbath. Fifth and Cheaper Edition. Crown 8vo, 5*s.*

Arrows in the Air. Fifth and Cheaper Edition. Crown 8vo, 5*s.*

Speech in Season. Fifth and Cheaper Edition. Crown 8vo, 5*s.*

Thoughts for the Times. Thirteenth and Cheaper Edition. Crown 8vo, 5*s.*

Unsectarian Family Prayers. New and Cheaper Edition. Fcap. 8vo, 1*s.* 6*d.*

HAWKINS, Edwards Comerford.—**Spirit and Form.** Sermons preached in the Parish Church of Leatherhead. Crown 8vo, 6*s.*

HAWTHORNE, Nathaniel.—**Works.** Complete in Twelve Volumes. Large post 8vo, 7*s.* 6*d.* each volume.

VOL. I. TWICE-TOLD TALES.
II. MOSSES FROM AN OLD MANSE.
III. THE HOUSE OF THE SEVEN GABLES, AND THE SNOW IMAGE.
IV. THE WONDERBOOK, TANGLEWOOD TALES, AND GRAND-FATHER'S CHAIR.
V. THE SCARLET LETTER, AND THE BLITHEDALE ROMANCE.
VI. THE MARBLE FAUN. [Transformation.]
VII.⎱ OUR OLD HOME, AND ENGLISH NOTE-BOOKS.
VIII.⎰
IX. AMERICAN NOTE-BOOKS.
X. FRENCH AND ITALIAN NOTE-BOOKS.
XI. SEPTIMIUS FELTON, THE DOLLIVER ROMANCE, FANSHAWE, AND, IN AN APPENDIX, THE ANCESTRAL FOOTSTEP.
XII. TALES AND ESSAYS, AND OTHER PAPERS, WITH A BIO-GRAPHICAL SKETCH OF HAWTHORNE.

HAYES, A. H., Junr.—**New Colorado, and the Santa Fé Trail.** With Map and 60 Illustrations. Crown 8vo, 9*s.*

HENNESSY, Sir John Pope.—**Ralegh in Ireland.** With his Letters on Irish Affairs and some Contemporary Documents. Large crown 8vo, printed on hand-made paper, parchment, 10*s.* 6*d.*

HENRY, Philip.—**Diaries and Letters of.** Edited by MATTHEW HENRY LEE, M.A. Large crown 8vo, 7*s.* 6*d.*

HIDE, Albert.—**The Age to Come.** Small crown 8vo, 2*s.* 6*d.*

HIME, Major H. W. L., R.A.—**Wagnerism : A Protest.** Crown 8vo, 2s. 6d.

HINTON, J.—**Life and Letters.** Edited by ELLICE HOPKINS, with an Introduction by Sir W. W. GULL, Bart., and Portrait engraved on Steel by C. H. Jeens. Fourth Edition. Crown 8vo, 8s. 6d.

The Mystery of Pain. New Edition. Fcap. 8vo, 1s.

HOLTHAM, E. G.—**Eight Years in Japan, 1873-1881.** Work, Travel, and Recreation. With three maps. Large crown 8vo, 9s.

HOOPER, Mary.—**Little Dinners: How to Serve them with Elegance and Economy.** Seventeenth Edition. Crown 8vo, 2s. 6d.

Cookery for Invalids, Persons of Delicate Digestion, and Children. Third Edition. Crown 8vo, 2s. 6d.

Every-Day Meals. Being Economical and Wholesome Recipes for Breakfast, Luncheon, and Supper. Fifth Edition. Crown 8vo, 2s. 6d.

HOPKINS, Ellice.—**Life and Letters of James Hinton,** with an Introduction by Sir W. W. GULL, Bart., and Portrait engraved on Steel by C. H. Jeens. Fourth Edition. Crown 8vo, 8s. 6d.

Work amongst Working Men. Fourth edition. Crown 8vo, 3s. 6d.

HOSPITALIER, E.—**The Modern Applications of Electricity.** Translated and Enlarged by JULIUS MAIER, Ph.D. 2 vols. With numerous Illustrations. Demy 8vo, 12s. 6d. each volume.
VOL. I.—Electric Generators, Electric Light.
VOL. II.—Telephone : Various Applications : Electrical Transmission of Energy.

Household Readings on Prophecy. By a Layman. Small crown 8vo, 3s. 6d.

HUGHES, Henry.—**The Redemption of the World.** Crown 8vo, 3s. 6d.

HUNTINGFORD, Rev. E., D.C.L.—**The Apocalypse.** With a Commentary and Introductory Essay. Demy 8vo, 9s.

HUTTON, Arthur, M.A.—**The Anglican Ministry :** Its Nature and Value in relation to the Catholic Priesthood. With a Preface by His Eminence CARDINAL NEWMAN. Demy 8vo, 14s.

HUTTON, Rev. C. F.—**Unconscious Testimony ;** or, the Silent Witness of the Hebrew to the Truth of the Historical Scriptures. Crown 8vo, 2s. 6d.

IM THURN, Everard F.—**Among the Indians of British Guiana.** Being Sketches, chiefly anthropologic, from the Interior of British Guiana. With numerous Illustrations. Demy 8vo.

JENKINS, E., and RAYMOND, J.—The Architect's Legal Handbook. Third Edition, Revised. Crown 8vo, 6s.

JENKINS, Rev. R. C., M.A.—The Privilege of Peter, and the Claims of the Roman Church confronted with the Scriptures, the Councils, and the Testimony of the Popes themselves. Fcap. 8vo, 3s. 6d.

JERVIS, Rev. W. Henley.—The Gallican Church and the Revolution. A Sequel to the History of the Church of France, from the Concordat of Bologna to the Revolution. Demy 8vo, 18s.

JOEL, L.—A Consul's Manual and Shipowner's and Shipmaster's Practical Guide in their Transactions Abroad. With Definitions of Nautical, Mercantile, and Legal Terms; a Glossary of Mercantile Terms in English, French, German, Italian, and Spanish; Tables of the Money, Weights, and Measures of the Principal Commercial Nations and their Equivalents in British Standards; and Forms of Consular and Notarial Acts. Demy 8vo, 12s.

JOHNSTONE, C. F., M.A.—Historical Abstracts: being Outlines of the History of some of the less known States of Europe. Crown 8vo, 7s. 6d.

JOLLY, William, F.R.S.E., etc.—The Life of John Duncan, Scotch Weaver and Botanist. With Sketches of his Friends and Notices of his Times. Second Edition. Large crown 8vo, with etched portrait, 9s.

JONES, C. A.—The Foreign Freaks of Five Friends. With 30 Illustrations. Crown 8vo, 6s.

JOYCE, P. W., LL.D., etc.—Old Celtic Romances. Translated from the Gaelic. Crown 8vo, 7s. 6d.

JOYNES, J. L.—The Adventures of a Tourist in Ireland. Second edition. Small crown 8vo, 2s. 6d.

KAUFMANN, Rev. M., B.A.—Socialism: its Nature, its Dangers, and its Remedies considered. Crown 8vo, 7s. 6d.

Utopias; or, Schemes of Social Improvement, from Sir Thomas More to Karl Marx. Crown 8vo, 5s.

KAY, Joseph.—Free Trade in Land. Edited by his Widow. With Preface by the Right Hon. JOHN BRIGHT, M.P. Sixth Edition. Crown 8vo, 5s.

KEMPIS, Thomas à.—Of the Imitation of Christ. Parchment Library Edition, 6s.; or vellum, 7s. 6d. The Red Line Edition, fcap. 8vo, red edges, 2s. 6d. The Cabinet Edition, small 8vo, cloth limp, 1s.; cloth boards, red edges, 1s. 6d. The Miniature Edition, red edges, 32mo, 1s.

*** All the above Editions may be had in various extra bindings

KENT, C.—Corona Catholica ad Petri successoris Pede. Oblata: De Summi Pontificis Leonis XIII. Assumptione Epigramma. In Quinquaginta Linguis. Fcap. 4to, 15s.

KETTLEWELL, Rev. S.—Thomas à Kempis and the Brothers of Common Life. 2 vols. With Frontispieces. Demy 8vo, 30s.

KIDD, Joseph, M.D.—The Laws of Therapeutics; or, the Science and Art of Medicine. Second Edition. Crown 8vo, 6s.

KINGSFORD, Anna, M.D.—The Perfect Way in Diet. A Treatise advocating a Return to the Natural and Ancient Food of our Race. Small crown 8vo, 2s.

KINGSLEY, Charles, M.A.—Letters and Memories of his Life. Edited by his Wife. With two Steel Engraved Portraits, and Vignettes on Wood. Thirteenth Cabinet Edition. 2 vols. Crown 8vo, 12s.

　　*** Also a New and Condensed Edition, in one volume. With Portrait. Crown 8vo, 6s.

　　All Saints' Day, and other Sermons. Also a new and condensed Edition in one volume, with Portrait. Crown 8vo, 6s. Edited by the Rev. W. HARRISON. Third Edition. Crown 8vo, 7s. 6d.

　　True Words for Brave Men. A Book for Soldiers' and Sailors' Libraries. Tenth Edition. Crown 8vo, 2s. 6d.

KNOX, Alexander A.—The New Playground; or, Wanderings in Algeria. New and cheaper edition. Large crown 8vo, 6s.

LANDON Joseph.—School Management; Including a General View of the Work of Education, Organization, and Discipline. Second Edition. Crown 8vo, 6s.

LAURIE, S. S.—The Training of Teachers, and other Educational Papers. Crown 8vo, 7s. 6d.

LEE, Rev. F. G., D.C.L.—The Other World; or, Glimpses of the Supernatural. 2 vols. A New Edition. Crown 8vo, 15s.

Letters from a Young Emigrant in Manitoba. Second Edition. Small crown 8vo, 3s. 6d.

LEWIS, Edward Dillon.—A Draft Code of Criminal Law and Procedure. Demy 8vo, 21s.

LILLIE, Arthur, M.R.A.S.—The Popular Life of Buddha. Containing an Answer to the Hibbert Lectures of 1881. With Illustrations. Crown 8vo, 6s.

LINDSAY, W. Lauder, M.D.—Mind in the Lower Animals in Health and Disease. 2 vols. Demy 8vo, 32s.
　　Vol. I.—Mind in Health. Vol. II.—Mind in Disease.

LLOYD, Walter.—The Hope of the World: An Essay on Universal Redemption. Crown 8vo, 5s.

LONSDALE, Margaret.—Sister Dora: a Biography. With Portrait. Twenty-fifth Edition. Crown 8vo, 2s. 6d.

LOWDER, Charles.—A Biography. By the Author of "St. Teresa." New and Cheaper Edition. Crown 8vo. With Portrait. 3s. 6d.

LYTTON, Edward Bulwer, Lord.—**Life, Letters and Literary Remains.** By his Son, The EARL OF LYTTON. With Portraits, Illustrations and Facsimiles. Demy 8vo.

[Vols. I. and II. just ready.

MACHIAVELLI, Niccolò.—**Discourses on the First Decade of Titus Livius.** Translated from the Italian by NINIAN HILL THOMSON, M.A. Large crown 8vo, 12s.

The Prince. Translated from the Italian by N. H. T. Small crown 8vo, printed on hand-made paper, bevelled boards, 6s.

MACKENZIE, Alexander.—**How India is Governed.** Being an Account of England's Work in India. Small crown 8vo, 2s.

MACNAUGHT, Rev. John.—**Cœna Domini :** An Essay on the Lord's Supper, its Primitive Institution, Apostolic Uses, and Subsequent History. Demy 8vo, 14s.

MACWALTER, Rev. G. S.—**Life of Antonis Rosmini Serbati** (Founder of the Institute of Charity). 2 vols. Demy 8vo.

[Vol. I. now ready, price 12s.

MAGNUS, Mrs.—**About the Jews since Bible Times.** From the Babylonian Exile till the English Exodus. Small crown 8vo, 6s.

MAIR, R. S., M.D., F.R.C.S.E.—**The Medical Guide for Anglo-Indians.** Being a Compendium of Advice to Europeans in India, relating to the Preservation and Regulation of Health. With a Supplement on the Management of Children in India. Second Edition. Crown 8vo, limp cloth, 3s. 6d.

MALDEN, Henry Elliot.—**Vienna, 1683.** The History and Consequences of the Defeat of the Turks before Vienna, September 12th, 1683, by John Sobieski, King of Poland, and Charles Leopold, Duke of Lorraine. Crown 8vo, 4s. 6d.

Many Voices. A volume of Extracts from the Religious Writers of Christendom from the First to the Sixteenth Century. With Biographical Sketches. Crown 8vo, cloth extra, red edges, 6s.

MARKHAM, Capt. Albert Hastings, R.N.—**The Great Frozen Sea :** A Personal Narrative of the Voyage of the *Alert* during the Arctic Expedition of 1875–6. With 6 Full-page Illustrations, 2 Maps, and 27 Woodcuts. Sixth and Cheaper Edition. Crown 8vo, 6s.

A Polar Reconnaissance : being the Voyage of the *Isbjörn* to Novaya Zemlya in 1879. With 10 Illustrations. Demy 8vo, 16s.

Marriage and Maternity ; or, Scripture Wives and Mothers. Small crown 8vo, 4s. 6d.

MARTINEAU, Gertrude.—**Outline Lessons on Morals.** Small crown 8vo, 3s. 6d.

MAUDSLEY, H., M.D.—**Body and Will.** Being an Essay concerning Will, in its Metaphysical, Physiological, and Pathological Aspects. 8vo, 12s.

McGRATH, Terence.—Pictures from Ireland. New and Cheaper Edition. Crown 8vo, 2s.

MEREDITH, M.A.—Theotokos, the Example for Woman. Dedicated, by permission, to Lady Agnes Wood. Revised by the Venerable Archdeacon DENISON. 32mo, limp cloth, 1s. 6d.

MILLER, Edward.—The History and Doctrines of Irvingism; or, the so-called Catholic and Apostolic Church. 2 vols. Large post 8vo, 25s.

The Church in Relation to the State. Large crown 8vo, 7s. 6d.

MINCHIN, J. G.—Bulgaria since the War: Notes of a Tour in the Autumn of 1879. Small crown 8vo, 3s. 6d.

MITFORD, Bertram.—Through the Zulu Country. Its Battle-fields and its People. With five Illustrations. Demy 8vo, 14s.

MIVART, St. George.—Nature and Thought: An Introduction to a Natural Philosophy. Demy 8vo, 10s. 6d.

MOCKLER, E.—A Grammar of the Baloochee Language, as it is spoken in Makran (Ancient Gedrosia), in the Persia-Arabic and Roman characters. Fcap. 8vo, 5s.

MOLESWORTH, Rev. W. Nassau, M.A.—History of the Church of England from 1660. Large crown 8vo, 7s. 6d.

MORELL, J. R.—Euclid Simplified in Method and Language. Being a Manual of Geometry. Compiled from the most important French Works, approved by the University of Paris and the Minister of Public Instruction. Fcap. 8vo, 2s. 6d.

MORSE, E. S., Ph.D.—First Book of Zoology. With numerous Illustrations. New and Cheaper Edition. Crown 8vo, 2s. 6d.

MURPHY, John Nicholas.—The Chair of Peter; or, the Papacy considered in its Institution, Development, and Organization, and in the Benefits which for over Eighteen Centuries it has conferred on Mankind. Demy 8vo, 18s.

NELSON, J. H., M.A.—A Prospectus of the Scientific Study of the Hindû Law. Demy 8vo, 9s.

NEWMAN, J. H., D.D.—Characteristics from the Writings of. Being Selections from his various Works. Arranged with the Author's personal Approval. Sixth Edition. With Portrait. Crown 8vo, 6s.

*** A Portrait of Cardinal Newman, mounted for framing, can be had, 2s. 6d.

NEWMAN, Francis William.—Essays on Diet. Small crown 8vo, cloth limp, 2s.

New Werther. By LOKI. Small crown 8vo, 2s. 6d.

NICHOLSON, Edward Byron.—**The Gospel according to the Hebrews.** Its Fragments Translated and Annotated with a Critical Analysis of the External and Internal Evidence relating to it. Demy 8vo, 9s. 6d.

A New Commentary on the Gospel according to Matthew. Demy 8vo, 12s.

NICOLS, Arthur, F.G.S., F.R.G.S.—**Chapters from the Physical History of the Earth:** an Introduction to Geology and Palæontology. With numerous Illustrations. Crown 8vo, 5s.

NOPS, Marianne.—**Class Lessons on Euclid.** Part I. containing the First two Books of the Elements. Crown 8vo, 2s. 6d.

Notes on St. Paul's Epistle to the Galatians. For Readers of the Authorized Version or the Original Greek. Demy 8vo, 2s. 6d.

Nuces: EXERCISES ON THE SYNTAX OF THE PUBLIC SCHOOL LATIN PRIMER. New Edition in Three Parts. Crown 8vo, each 1s.
₊ The Three Parts can also be had bound together, 3s.

OATES, Frank, F.R.G.S.—**Matabele Land and the Victoria Falls.** A Naturalist's Wanderings in the Interior of South Africa. Edited by C. G. OATES, B.A. With numerous Illustrations and 4 Maps. Demy 8vo, 21s.

OGLE, W., M.D., F.R.C.P.—**Aristotle on the Parts of Animals.** Translated, with Introduction and Notes. Royal 8vo, 12s. 6d.

Oken Lorenz, Life of. By ALEXANDER ECKER. With Explanatory Notes, Selections from Oken's Correspondence, and Portrait of the Professor. From the German by ALFRED TULK. Crown 8vo, 6s.

O'MEARA, Kathleen.—**Frederic Ozanam,** Professor of the Sorbonne: His Life and Work. Second Edition. Crown 8vo, 7s. 6d.

Henri Perreyve and his Counsels to the Sick. Small crown 8vo, 5s.

OSBORNE, Rev. W. A.—**The Revised Version of the New Testament.** A Critical Commentary, with Notes upon the Text. Crown 8vo, 5s.

OTTLEY, H. Bickersteth.—**The Great Dilemma.** Christ His Own Witness or His Own Accuser. Six Lectures. Second Edition. Crown 8vo, 3s. 6d.

Our Public Schools—Eton, Harrow, Winchester, Rugby, Westminster, Marlborough, The Charterhouse. Crown 8vo, 6s.

OWEN, F. M.—**John Keats:** a Study. Crown 8vo, 6s.

OWEN, Rev. Robert, B.D.—**Sanctorale Catholicum;** or, Book of Saints. With Notes, Critical, Exegetical, and Historical. Demy 8vo, 18s.

OXENHAM, *Rev. F. Nutcombe.*—What is the Truth as to Ever-lasting Punishment. Part II. Being an Historical Inquiry into the Witness and Weight of certain Anti-Origenist Councils. Crown 8vo, 2s. 6d.

OXONIENSES.—Romanism, Protestantism, Anglicanism. Being a Layman's View of some questions of the Day. Together with Remarks on Dr. Littledale's "Plain Reasons against join-ing the Church of Rome." Crown 8vo, 3s. 6d.

PALMER, *the late William.*—Notes of a Visit to Russia in 1840–1841. Selected and arranged by JOHN H. CARDINAL NEWMAN, with portrait. Crown 8vo, 8s. 6d.

Parchment Library. Choicely Printed on hand-made paper, limp parchment antique, 6s. ; vellum, 7s. 6d. each volume.

English Lyrics.

The Sonnets of John Milton. Edited by MARK PATTISON. With Portrait after Vertue.

Poems by Alfred Tennyson. 2 vols. With minature frontis-pieces by W. B. Richmond.

French Lyrics. Selected and Annotated by GEORGE SAINTS-BURY. With a minature frontispiece designed and etched by H. G. Glindoni.

The Fables of Mr. John Gay. With Memoir by AUSTIN DOBSON, and an etched portrait from an unfinished Oil Sketch by Sir Godfrey Kneller.

Select Letters of Percy Bysshe Shelley. Edited, with an Introduction, by RICHARD GARNETT.

The Christian Year. Thoughts in Verse for the Sundays and Holy Days throughout the Year. With Miniature Portrait of the Rev. J. Keble, after a Drawing by G. Richmond, R.A.

Shakspere's Works. Complete in Twelve Volumes.

Eighteenth Century Essays. Selected and Edited by AUSTIN DOBSON. With a Miniature Frontispiece by R. Caldecott.

Q. Horati Flacci Opera. Edited by F. A. CORNISH, Assistant Master at Eton. With a Frontispiece after a design by L. Alma Tadema, etched by Leopold Lowenstam.

Edgar Allan Poe's Poems. With an Essay on his Poetry by ANDREW LANG, and a Frontispiece by Linley Sambourne.

Shakspere's Sonnets. Edited by EDWARD DOWDEN. With a Frontispiece etched by Leopold Lowenstam, after the Death Mask.

English Odes. Selected by EDMUND W. GOSSE. With Frontis-piece on India paper by Hamo Thornycroft, A.R.A.

Of the Imitation of Christ. By THOMAS À KEMPIS. A revised Translation. With Frontispiece on India paper, from a Design by W. B. Richmond.

Parchment Library—*continued.*

    Tennyson's The Princess: a Medley. With a Miniature Frontispiece by H. M. Paget, and a Tailpiece in Outline by Gordon Browne.

    Poems: Selected from PERCY BYSSHE SHELLEY. Dedicated to Lady Shelley. With a Preface by RICHARD GARNETT and a Miniature Frontispiece.

    Tennyson's "In Memoriam." With a Miniature Portrait in *eau-forte* by Le Rat, after a Photograph by the late Mrs. Cameron.

PARSLOE, Joseph.—**Our Railways.** Sketches, Historical and Descriptive. With Practical Information as to Fares and Rates, etc., and a Chapter on Railway Reform. Crown 8vo, 6s.

PAUL, C. Kegan.—**Biographical Sketches,** Printed on hand-made paper, bound in buckram. Second Edition. Crown 8vo, 7s. 6d.

PAUL, Alexander.—**Short Parliaments.** A History of the National Demand for frequent General Elections. Small crown 8vo, 3s. 6d.

PEARSON, Rev. S.—**Week-day Living.** A Book for Young Men and Women. Second Edition. Crown 8vo, 5s.

PENRICE, Maj. J., B.A.—**A Dictionary and Glossary of the Ko-ran.** With Copious Grammatical References and Explanations of the Text. 4to, 21s.

PESCHEL, Dr. Oscar.—**The Races of Man and their Geographical Distribution.** Large crown 8vo, 9s.

PETERS, F. H.—**The Nicomachean Ethics of Aristotle.** Translated by. Crown 8vo, 6s.

PHIPSON, E.—**The Animal Lore of Shakspeare's Time.** Including Quadrupeds, Birds, Reptiles, Fish and Insects. Large post 8vo, 9s.

PIDGEON, D.—**An Engineer's Holiday;** or, Notes of a Round Trip from Long. 0° to 0°. New and Cheaper Edition. Large crown 8vo, 7s. 6d.

PRICE, Prof. Bonamy.—**Currency and Banking.** Crown 8vo, 6s.

    Chapters on Practical Political Economy. Being the Substance of Lectures delivered before the University of Oxford. New and Cheaper Edition. Large post 8vo, 5s.

Pulpit Commentary, The. (Old Testament Series.) Edited by the Rev. J. S. EXELL and the Rev. Canon H. D. M. SPENCE.

    Genesis. By the Rev. T. WHITELAW, M.A.; with Homilies by the Very Rev. J. F. MONTGOMERY, D.D., Rev. Prof. R. A. REDFORD, M.A., LL.B., Rev. F. HASTINGS, Rev. W. ROBERTS, M.A. An Introduction to the Study of the Old Testament by the Venerable Archdeacon FARRAR, D.D., F.R.S.; and Introductions to the Pentateuch by the Right Rev. H. COTTERILL, D.D., and Rev. T. WHITELAW, M.A. Seventh Edition. 1 vol., 15s.

Pulpit Commentary, The—*continued.*

Exodus. By the Rev. Canon RAWLINSON. With Homilies by Rev. J. ORR, Rev. D. YOUNG, Rev. C. A. GOODHART, Rev. J. URQUHART, and the Rev. H. T. ROBJOHNS. Third Edition. 2 vols., 18s.

Leviticus. By the Rev. Prebendary MEYRICK, M.A. With Introductions by the Rev. R. COLLINS, Rev. Professor A. CAVE, and Homilies by Rev. Prof. REDFORD, LL.B., Rev. J. A. MACDONALD, Rev. W. CLARKSON, Rev. S. R. ALDRIDGE, LL.B., and Rev. McCHEYNE EDGAR. Fourth Edition. 15s.

Numbers. By the Rev. R. WINTERBOTHAM, LL.B.; with Homilies by the Rev. Professor W. BINNIE, D.D., Rev. E. S. PROUT, M.A., Rev. D. YOUNG, Rev. J. WAITE, and an Introduction by the Rev. THOMAS WHITELAW, M.A. Fourth Edition. 15s.

Deuteronomy. By the Rev. W. L. ALEXANDER, D.D. With Homilies by Rev. C. CLEMANCE, D.D., Rev. J. ORR, B.D., Rev. R. M. EDGAR, M.A., Rev. D. DAVIES, M.A. Third edition. 15s.

Joshua. By Rev. J. J. LIAS, M.A.; with Homilies by Rev. S. R. ALDRIDGE, LL.B., Rev. R. GLOVER, REV. E. DE PRESSENSÉ, D.D., Rev. J. WAITE, B.A., Rev. F. W. ADENEY, M.A.; and an Introduction by the Rev. A. PLUMMER, M.A. Fifth Edition. 12s. 6d.

Judges and Ruth. By the Bishop of Bath and Wells, and Rev. J. MORRISON, D.D.; with Homilies by Rev. A. F. MUIR, M.A., Rev. W. F. ADENEY, M.A., Rev. W. M. STATHAM, and Rev. Professor J. THOMSON, M.A. Fourth Edition. 10s. 6d.

1 Samuel. By the Very Rev. R. P. SMITH, D.D.; with Homilies by Rev. DONALD FRASER, D.D., Rev. Prof. CHAPMAN, and Rev. B. DALE. Sixth Edition. 15s.

1 Kings. By the Rev. JOSEPH HAMMOND, LL.B. With Homilies by the Rev. E. DE PRESSENSÉ, D.D., Rev. J. WAITE, B.A., Rev. A. ROWLAND, LL.B., Rev. J. A. MACDONALD, and Rev. J. URQUHART. Fourth Edition. 15s.

Ezra, Nehemiah, and Esther. By Rev. Canon G. RAWLINSON, M.A.; with Homilies by Rev. Prof. J. R. THOMSON, M.A., Rev. Prof. R. A. REDFORD, LL.B., M.A., Rev. W. S. LEWIS, M.A., Rev. J. A. MACDONALD, Rev. A. MACKENNAL, B.A., Rev. W. CLARKSON, B.A., Rev. F. HASTINGS, Rev. W. DINWIDDIE, LL.B., Rev. Prof. ROWLANDS, B.A., Rev. G. WOOD, B.A., Rev. Prof. P. C. BARKER, LL.B., M.A., and the Rev. J. S. EXELL. Sixth Edition. 1 vol., 12s. 6d.

Jeremiah. By the Rev. J. K. CHEYNE, M.A.; with Homilies by the Rev. W. F. ADENEY, M.A., Rev. A. F. MUIR, M.A., Rev. S. CONWAY, B.A., Rev. J. WAITE, B.A., and Rev. D. YOUNG, B.A. Vol. I., 15s.

Pulpit Commentary, The. (New Testament Series.)
St. Mark. By Very Rev. E. BICKERSTETH, D.D., Dean of Lich-field ; with Homilies by Rev. Prof. THOMSON, M.A., Rev. Prof. GIVEN, M.A., Rev. Prof. JOHNSON, M.A., Rev. A. ROWLAND, B.A., LL.B., Rev. A. MUIR, and Rev. R. GREEN. **2 vols.** Third Edition. *21s.*

PUSEY, Dr.—**Sermons for the Church's Seasons from Advent to Trinity.** Selected from the Published Sermons of the late EDWARD BOUVERIE PUSEY, D.D. Crown 8vo, *5s.*

QUILTER, Harry.—**"The Academy," 1872-1882.**

RADCLIFFE, Frank R. Y.—**The New Politicus.** Small crown 8vo, *2s. 6d.*

Realities of the Future Life. Small crown 8vo, *1s. 6d.*

RENDELL, J. M.—**Concise Handbook of the Island of Madeira.** With Plan of Funchal and Map of the Island. Fcap. 8vo, *1s. 6d.*

REYNOLDS, Rev. J. W.—**The Supernatural in Nature.** A Verification by Free Use of Science. Third Edition, Revised and Enlarged. Demy 8vo, *14s.*

The Mystery of Miracles. Third and Enlarged Edition. Crown 8vo, *6s.*

RIBOT, Prof. Th.—**Heredity:** A Psychological Study on its Phenomena, its Laws, its Causes, and its Consequences. Large crown 8vo, *9s.*

ROBERTSON, The late Rev. F. W., M.A.—**Life and Letters of.** Edited by the Rev. STOPFORD BROOKE, M.A.
I. Two vols., uniform with the Sermons. With Steel Portrait. Crown 8vo, *7s. 6d.*
II. Library Edition, in Demy 8vo, with Portrait. *12s.*
III. A Popular Edition, in 1 vol. Crown 8vo, *6s.*

Sermons. Four Series. Small crown 8vo, *3s. 6d.* each.

The Human Race, and other Sermons. Preached at Chelten-ham, Oxford, and Brighton. New and Cheaper Edition. Crown 8vo, *3s. 6d.*

Notes on Genesis. New and Cheaper Edition. Crown 8vo, *3s. 6d.*

Expository Lectures on St. Paul's Epistles to the Corinthians. A New Edition. Small crown 8vo, *5s.*

Lectures and Addresses, with other Literary Remains. A New Edition. Crown 8vo, *5s.*

An Analysis of Mr. Tennyson's "In Memoriam." (Dedicated by Permission to the Poet-Laureate.) Fcap. 8vo, *2s.*

The Education of the Human Race. Translated from the German of GOTTHOLD EPHRAIM LESSING. Fcap. 8vo, *2s. 6d.*

The above Works can also be had, bound in half morocco.

₊₊* A Portrait of the late Rev. F. W. Robertson, mounted for framing, can be had, *2s. 6d.*

Rosmini Serbati (Life of). By G. STUART MACWALTER. 2 vols. 8vo. [Vol. I. now ready, 12s.

Rosmini's Origin of Ideas. Translated from the Fifth Italian Edition of the Nuovo Saggio *Sull' origine delle idee.* 3 vols. Demy 8vo, cloth. [Vols. I. and II. now ready, 16s. each.

Rosmini's Philosophical System. Translated, with a Sketch of the Author's Life, Bibliography, Introduction, and Notes by THOMAS DAVIDSON. Demy 8vo, 16s.

RULE, Martin, M.A.—**The Life and Times of St. Anselm, Archbishop of Canterbury and Primate of the Britains.** 2 vols. Demy 8vo, 21s.

SALVATOR, Archduke Ludwig.—**Levkosia, the Capital of Cyprus.** Crown 4to, 10s. 6d.

SAMUEL, Sydney M.—**Jewish Life in the East.** Small crown 8vo, 3s. 6d.

SAYCE, Rev. Archibald Henry.—**Introduction to the Science of Language.** 2 vols. Second Edition. Large post 8vo, 25s.

Scientific Layman. The New Truth and the Old Faith : are they Incompatible ? Demy 8vo, 10s. 6d.

SCOONES, W. Baptiste.—**Four Centuries of English Letters :** A Selection of 350 Letters by 150 Writers, from the Period of the Paston Letters to the Present Time. Third Edition. Large crown 8vo, 6s.

SHILLITO, Rev. Joseph.—**Womanhood** : its Duties, Temptations and Privileges. A Book for Young Women. Third Edition Crown 8vo, 3s. 6d.

SHIPLEY, Rev. Orby, M.A.—**Principles of the Faith in Relation to Sin.** Topics for Thought in Times of Retreat Eleven Addresses delivered during a Retreat of Three Days to Persons living in the World. Demy 8vo, 12s.

Sister Augustine, Superior of the Sisters of Charity at the St Johannis Hospital at Bonn. Authorised Translation by HANS THARAU, from the German "Memorials of AMALIE VON LASAULX." Cheap Edition. Large crown 8vo, 4s. 6d.

SMITH, Edward, M.D., LL.B., F.R.S.—**Tubercular Consumption in its Early and Remediable Stages.** Second Edition. Crown 8vo, 6s.

SPEDDING, James.—**Reviews and Discussions, Literary Political, and Historical not relating to Bacon.** Demy 8vo, 12s. 6d.

Evenings with a Reviewer ; or, Bacon and Macaulay With a Prefatory Notice by G. S. VENABLES, Q.C. 2 vols Demy 8vo, 18s.

STAPFER, Paul.—Shakspeare and Classical Antiquity : Greek and Latin Antiquity as presented in Shakspeare's Plays. Translated by EMILY J. CAREY. Large post 8vo, 12*s.*

STEVENSON, Rev. W. F.—Hymns for the Church and Home. Selected and Edited by the Rev. W. FLEMING STEVENSON.

The Hymn Book consists of Three Parts :—I. For Public Worship.—II. For Family and Private Worship.—III. For Children.

*** Published in various forms and prices, the latter ranging from 8*d.* to 6*s.*

Lists and full particulars will be furnished on application to the Publishers.

STEVENSON, Robert Louis.—Travels with a Donkey in the Cevennes. With Frontispiece by Walter Crane. Small crown 8vo, 2*s.* 6*d.*

An Inland Voyage. With Frontispiece by Walter Crane. Small Crown 8vo, 2*s.* 6*d.*

Virginibus Puerisque, and other Papers. Crown 8vo, 6*s.*

Stray Papers on Education, and Scenes from School Life. By B. H. Small crown 8vo, 3*s.* 6*d.*

STRECKER-WISLICENUS.—Organic Chemistry. Translated and Edited, with Extensive Additions, by W. R. HODGKINSON, Ph.D., and A. J. GREENAWAY, F.I.C. Demy 8vo, 21*s.*

SULLY, James, M.A.—Pessimism : a History and a Criticism. Second Edition. Demy 8vo, 14*s.*

SWEDENBORG, Eman.—De Cultu et Amore Dei ubi Agitur de Telluris ortu, Paradiso et Vivario, tum de Primogeniti Seu Adami Nativitate Infantia, et Amore. Crown 8vo, 5*s.*

SYME, David.—Representative Government in England. Its Faults and Failures. Second Edition. Large crown 8vo, 6*s.*

TAYLOR, Rev. Isaac.—The Alphabet. An Account of the Origin and Development of Letters. With numerous Tables and Facsimiles. 2 vols. Demy 8vo, 36*s.*

Thirty Thousand Thoughts. Edited by the Rev. CANON SPENCE, Rev. J. S. EXELL, Rev. CHARLES NEIL, and Rev. JACOB STEPHENSON. 6 vols. Super royal 8vo.

[Vol. I. now ready, 16*s.*

THOM, J. Hamilton.—Laws of Life after the Mind of Christ. Second Edition. Crown 8vo, 7*s.* 6*d.*

THOMSON, J. Turnbull.—Social Problems ; or, An Inquiry into the Laws of Influence. With Diagrams. Demy 8vo, 10*s.* 6*d.*

TIDMAN, Paul F.—Gold and Silver Money. Part I.—A Plain Statement. Part II.—Objections Answered. Third Edition. Crown 8vo, 1s.

TIPPLE, Rev. S. A.—Sunday Mornings at Norwood. Prayers and Sermons. Crown 8vo, 6s.

TODHUNTER, Dr. J.—A Study of Shelley. Crown 8vo, 7s.

TREMENHEERE, Hugh Seymour, C.B.—A Manual of the Principles of Government, as set forth by the Authorities of Ancient and Modern Times. New and Enlarged Edition. Crown 8vo, 5s.

TUKE, Daniel Hack, M.D., F.R.C.P.—Chapters in the History of the Insane in the British Isles. With 4 Illustrations. Large crown 8vo, 12s.

TWINING, Louisa.—Workhouse Visiting and Management during Twenty-Five Years. Small crown 8vo, 3s. 6d.

TYLER, J.—The Mystery of Being: or, What Do We Know? Small crown 8vo, 3s. 6d.

UPTON, Major R. D.—Gleanings from the Desert of Arabia. Large post 8vo, 10s. 6d.

VACUUS, Viator.—Flying South. Recollections of France and its Littoral. Small crown 8vo, 3s. 6d.

VAUGHAN, H. Halford.—New Readings and Renderings of Shakespeare's Tragedies. 2 vols. Demy 8vo, 25s.

VILLARI, Professor.—Niccolò Machiavelli and his Times. Translated by Linda Villari. 4 vols. Large post 8vo, 48s.

VILLIERS, The Right Hon. C. P.—Free Trade Speeches of. With Political Memoir. Edited by a Member of the Cobden Club. 2 vols. With Portrait. Demy 8vo, 25s.

VOGT, Lieut.-Col. Hermann.—The Egyptian War of 1882. A translation. With Map and Plans. Large crown 8vo, 6s.

VOLCKXSOM, E. W. V.—Catechism of Elementary Modern Chemistry. Small crown 8vo, 3s.

VYNER, Lady Mary.—Every Day a Portion. Adapted from the Bible and the Prayer Book, for the Private Devotion of those living in Widowhood. Collected and Edited by Lady Mary Vyner. Square crown 8vo, 5s.

WALDSTEIN, Charles, Ph.D.—The Balance of Emotion and Intellect; an Introductory Essay to the Study of Philosophy. Crown 8vo, 6s.

WALLER, Rev. C. B.—The Apocalypse, reviewed under the Light of the Doctrine of the Unfolding Ages, and the Restitution of All Things. Demy 8vo, 12s.

WALPOLE, Chas. George.—History of Ireland from the Earliest Times to the Union with Great Britain. With 5 Maps and Appendices. Crown 8vo, 10s. 6d.

WALSHE, Walter Hayle, M.D.—Dramatic Singing Physiologically Estimated. Crown 8vo, 3s. 6d.

WEDMORE, Frederick.—The Masters of Genre Painting. With Sixteen Illustrations. Crown 8vo, 7s. 6d.

WHEWELL, William, D.D.—His Life and Selections from his Correspondence. By Mrs. STAIR DOUGLAS. With a Portrait from a Painting by Samuel Laurence. Demy 8vo, 21s.

WHITNEY, Prof. William Dwight.—Essentials of English Grammar, for the Use of Schools. Crown 8vo, 3s. 6d.

WILLIAMS, Rowland, D.D.—Psalms, Litanies, Counsels, and Collects for Devout Persons. Edited by his Widow. New and Popular Edition. Crown 8vo, 3s. 6d.

Stray Thoughts Collected from the Writings of the late Rowland Williams, D.D. Edited by his Widow. Crown 8vo, 3s. 6d.

WILLIS, R., M.A.—William Harvey. A History of the Discovery of the Circulation of the Blood: with a Portrait of Harvey after Faithorne. Demy 8vo, 14s.

WILSON, Sir Erasmus.—Egypt of the Past. With Chromo-lithograph and numerous Illustrations in the text. Second Edition, Revised. Crown 8vo, 12s.

The Recent Archaic Discovery of Egyptian Mummies at Thebes. A Lecture. Crown 8vo, 1s. 6d.

WILSON, Lieut.-Col. C. T.—The Duke of Berwick, Marshall of France, 1702–1734. Demy 8vo, 15s.

WOLTMANN, Dr. Alfred, and WOERMANN, Dr. Karl.—History of Painting. Edited by SIDNEY COLVIN. Vol. I. Painting in Antiquity and the Middle Ages. With numerous Illustrations. Medium 8vo, 28s. ; bevelled boards, gilt leaves, 30s.

Word was Made Flesh. Short Family Readings on the Epistles for each Sunday of the Christian Year. Demy 8vo, 10s. 6d.

WREN, Sir Christopher.—His Family and His Times. With Original Letters, and a Discourse on Architecture hitherto unpublished. By LUCY PHILLIMORE. With Portrait. Demy 8vo, 14s.

YOUMANS, Eliza A.—First Book of Botany. Designed to Cultivate the Observing Powers of Children. With 300 Engravings. New and Cheaper Edition. Crown 8vo, 2s. 6d.

YOUMANS, Edward L., M.D.—A Class Book of Chemistry, on the Basis of the New System. With 200 Illustrations. Crown 8vo, 5s.

THE INTERNATIONAL SCIENTIFIC SERIES.

I. **Forms of Water**: a Familiar Exposition of the Origin and Phenomena of Glaciers. By J. Tyndall, LL.D., F.R.S. With 25 Illustrations. Eighth Edition. Crown 8vo, 5s.

II. **Physics and Politics**; or, Thoughts on the Application of the Principles of "Natural Selection" and "Inheritance" to Political Society. By Walter Bagehot. Sixth Edition. Crown 8vo, 4s.

III. **Foods.** By Edward Smith, M.D., LL.B., F.R.S. With numerous Illustrations. Eighth Edition. Crown 8vo, 5s.

IV. **Mind and Body**: the Theories of their Relation. By Alexander Bain, LL.D. With Four Illustrations. Seventh Edition. Crown 8vo, 4s.

V. **The Study of Sociology.** By Herbert Spencer. Eleventh Edition. Crown 8vo, 5s.

VI. **On the Conservation of Energy.** By Balfour Stewart, M.A., LL.D., F.R.S. With 14 Illustrations. Sixth Edition. Crown 8vo, 5s.

VII. **Animal Locomotion**; or Walking, Swimming, and Flying. By J. B. Pettigrew, M.D., F.R.S., etc. With 130 Illustrations. Third Edition. Crown 8vo, 5s.

VIII. **Responsibility in Mental Disease.** By Henry Maudsley, M.D. Fourth Edition. Crown 8vo, 5s.

IX. **The New Chemistry.** By Professor J. P. Cooke. With 31 Illustrations. Seventh Edition. Crown 8vo, 5s.

X. **The Science of Law.** By Professor Sheldon Amos. Fifth Edition. Crown 8vo, 5s.

XI. **Animal Mechanism**: a Treatise on Terrestrial and Aerial Locomotion. By Professor E. J. Marey. With 117 Illustrations. Third Edition. Crown 8vo, 5s.

XII. **The Doctrine of Descent and Darwinism.** By Professor Oscar Schmidt. With 26 Illustrations. Fifth Edition. Crown 8vo, 5s.

XIII. **The History of the Conflict between Religion and Science.** By J. W. Draper, M.D., LL.D. Seventeenth Edition. Crown 8vo, 5s.

XIV. **Fungi**: their Nature, Influences, Uses, etc. By M. C. Cooke, M.D., LL.D. Edited by the Rev. M. J. Berkeley, M.A., F.L.S. With numerous Illustrations. Third Edition. Crown 8vo, 5s.

XV. **The Chemical Effects of Light and Photography.** By Dr. Hermann Vogel. Translation thoroughly Revised. With 100 Illustrations. Fourth Edition. Crown 8vo, 5s.

XVI. **The Life and Growth of Language.** By Professor William Dwight Whitney. Fourth Edition. Crown 8vo, 5s.

XVII. **Money and the Mechanism of Exchange.** By W. Stanley Jevons, M.A., F.R.S. Sixth Edition. Crown 8vo, 5s.

XVIII. **The Nature of Light.** With a General Account of Physical Optics. By Dr. Eugene Lommel. With 188 Illustrations and a Table of Spectra in Chromo-lithography. Third Edition. Crown 8vo, 5s.

XIX. **Animal Parasites and Messmates.** By Monsieur Van Beneden. With 83 Illustrations. Third Edition. Crown 8vo, 5s.

XX. **Fermentation.** By Professor Schützenberger. With 28 Illustrations. Third Edition. Crown 8vo, 5s.

XXI. **The Five Senses of Man.** By Professor Bernstein. With 91 Illustrations. Fourth Edition. Crown 8vo, 5s.

XXII. **The Theory of Sound in its Relation to Music.** By Professor Pietro Blaserna. With numerous Illustrations. Third Edition. Crown 8vo, 5s.

XXIII. **Studies in Spectrum Analysis.** By J. Norman Lockyer, F.R.S. With six photographic Illustrations of Spectra, and numerous engravings on Wood. Third Edition. Crown 8vo, 6s. 6d.

XXIV. **A History of the Growth of the Steam Engine.** By Professor R. H. Thurston. With numerous Illustrations. Third Edition. Crown 8vo, 6s. 6d.

XXV. **Education as a Science.** By Alexander Bain, LL.D. Fourth Edition. Crown 8vo, 5s.

XXVI. **The Human Species.** By Professor A. de Quatrefages. Third Edition. Crown 8vo, 5s.

XXVII. **Modern Chromatics.** With Applications to Art and Industry. By Ogden N. Rood. With 130 original Illustrations. Second Edition. Crown 8vo, 5s.

XXVIII. **The Crayfish :** an Introduction to the Study of Zoology. By Professor T. H. Huxley. With 82 Illustrations. Third Edition. Crown 8vo, 5s.

XXIX. **The Brain as an Organ of Mind.** By H. Charlton Bastian, M.D. With numerous Illustrations. Third Edition. Crown 8vo, 5s.

XXX. **The Atomic Theory.** By Prof. Wurtz. Translated by G. Cleminshaw, F.C.S. Third Edition. Crown 8vo, 5s.

XXXI. **The Natural Conditions of Existence as they affect Animal Life.** By Karl Semper. With 2 Maps and 106 Woodcuts. Third Edition. Crown 8vo, 5s.

XXXII. **General Physiology of Muscles and Nerves.** By Prof. J. Rosenthal. Third Edition. With Illustrations. Crown 8vo, 5*s*.

XXXIII. **Sight :** an Exposition of the Principles of Monocular and Binocular Vision. By Joseph le Conte, LL.D. Second Edition. With 132 Illustrations. Crown 8vo, 5*s*.

XXXIV. **Illusions :** a Psychological Study. By James Sully. Second Edition. Crown 8vo, 5*s*.

XXXV. **Volcanoes : what they are and what they teach.** By Professor J. W. Judd, F.R.S. With 92 Illustrations on Wood. Second Edition. Crown 8vo, 5*s*.

XXXVI. **Suicide :** an Essay in Comparative Moral Statistics. By Prof. E. Morselli. Second Edition. With Diagrams. Crown 8vo, 5*s*.

XXXVII. **The Brain and its Functions.** By J. Luys. With Illustrations. Second Edition. Crown 8vo, 5*s*.

XXXVIII. **Myth and Science :** an Essay. By Tito Vignoli. Crown 8vo, 5*s*.

XXXIX. **The Sun.** By Professor Young. With Illustrations. Second Edition. Crown 8vo, 5*s*.

XL. **Ants, Bees, and Wasps :** a Record of Observations on the Habits of the Social Hymenoptera. By Sir John Lubbock, Bart., M.P. With 5 Chromo-lithographic Illustrations. Sixth Edition. Crown 8vo, 5*s*.

XLI. **Animal Intelligence.** By G. J. Romanes, LL.D., F.R.S. Third Edition. Crown 8vo, 5*s*.

XLII. **The Concepts and Theories of Modern Physics.** By J. B. Stallo. Second Edition. Crown 8vo, 5*s*.

XLIII. **Diseases of the Memory ;** An Essay in the Positive Psychology. By Prof. Th. Ribot. Second Edition. Crown 8vo, 5*s*.

XLIV. **Man before Metals.** By N. Joly, with 148 Illustrations. Third Edition. Crown 8vo, 5*s*.

XLV. **The Science of Politics.** By Prof. Sheldon Amos. Second Edition. Crown 8vo, 5*s*.

XLVI. **Elementary Meteorology.** By Robert H. Scott. Second Edition. With Numerous Illustrations. Crown 8vo, 5*s*.

XLVII. **The Organs of Speech and their Application in the Formation of Articulate Sounds.** By George Hermann Von Meyer. With 47 Woodcuts. Crown 8vo, 5*s*.

XLVIII. **Fallacies.** A View of Logic from the Practical Side. By Alfred Sidgwick.

MILITARY WORKS.

BARRINGTON, Capt. J. T.—England on the Defensive ; or, the Problem of Invasion Critically Examined. Large crown 8vo, with Map, 7*s.* 6*d.*

BRACKENBURY, Col. C. B., R.A., C.B.—Military Handbooks for Regimental Officers.

    I. Military Sketching and Reconnaissance. By Col. F. J. Hutchison, and Major H. G. MacGregor. Fourth Edition. With 15 Plates. Small 8vo, 6*s.*

    II. The Elements of Modern Tactics Practically applied to English Formations. By Lieut.-Col. Wilkinson Shaw. Fourth Edition. With 25 Plates and Maps. Small crown 8vo, 9*s.*

    III. Field Artillery. Its Equipment, Organization and Tactics. By Major Sisson C. Pratt, R.A. With 12 Plates. Second Edition. Small crown 8vo, 6*s.*

    IV. The Elements of Military Administration. First Part : Permanent System of Administration. By Major J. W. Buxton. Small crown 8vo. 7*s.* 6*d.*

    V. Military Law : Its Procedure and Practice. By Major Sisson C. Pratt, R.A. Small crown 8vo.

BROOKE, Major, C. K.—A System of Field Training. Small crown 8vo, cloth limp, 2*s.*

CLERY, C., Lieut.-Col.—Minor Tactics. With 26 Maps and Plans. Sixth and Cheaper Edition, Revised. Crown 8vo, 9*s.*

COLVILE, Lieut.-Col. C. F.—Military Tribunals. Sewed, 2*s.* 6*d.*

HARRISON, Lieut.-Col. R.—The Officer's Memorandum Book for Peace and War. Third Edition. Oblong 32mo, roan, with pencil, 3*s.* 6*d.*

Notes on Cavalry Tactics, Organisation, etc. By a Cavalry Officer. With Diagrams. Demy 8vo, 12*s.*

PARR, Capt. H. Hallam, C.M.G.—The Dress, Horses, and Equipment of Infantry and Staff Officers. Crown 8vo, 1*s.*

SCHAW, Col. H.—The Defence and Attack of Positions and Localities. Second Edition, Revised and Corrected. Crown 8vo, 3*s.* 6*d.*

SHADWELL, Maj.-Gen., C.B.—Mountain Warfare. Illustrated by the Campaign of 1799 in Switzerland. Being a Translation of the Swiss Narrative compiled from the Works of the Archduke Charles, Jomini, and others. Also of Notes by General H. Dufour on the Campaign of the Valtelline in 1635. With Appendix, Maps, and Introductory Remarks. Demy 8vo, 16*s.*

STUBBS, *Lieut.-Col. F. W.*—The Regiment of Bengal Artillery. The History of its Organisation, Equipment, and War Services. Compiled from Published Works, Official Records, and various Private Sources. With numerous Maps and Illustrations. **2 vols.** Demy 8vo, 32*s.*

POETRY.

ADAM OF ST. VICTOR.—The Liturgical Poetry of Adam of St. Victor. From the text of GAUTIER. With Translations into English in the Original Metres, and Short Explanatory Notes, by DIGBY S. WRANGHAM, M.A. 3 vols. Crown 8vo, printed on hand-made paper, boards, 21*s.*

AUCHMUTY, A. C.—Poems of English Heroism : From Brunanburh to Lucknow ; from Athelstan to Albert. Small crown 8vo, 1*s.* 6*d.*

AVIA.—The Odyssey of Homer. Done into English Verse by. Fcap. 4to, 15*s.*

BANKS, *Mrs. G. L.*—Ripples and Breakers : Poems. Square 8vo, 5*s.*

BARNES, *William.*—Poems of Rural Life, in the Dorset Dialect. New Edition, complete in one vol. Crown 8vo, 8*s.* 6*d.*

BAYNES, *Rev. Canon H. R.*—Home Songs for Quiet Hours. Fourth and Cheaper Edition. Fcap. 8vo, cloth, 2*s.* 6*d.*
⁎ This may also be had handsomely bound in morocco with gilt edges.

BENNETT, *C. Fletcher.*—Life Thoughts. A New Volume of Poems. With Frontispiece. Small crown 8vo.

BEVINGTON, L. S.—Key Notes. Small crown 8vo, 5*s.*

BILLSON, C. J.—The Acharnians of Aristophanes. Crown 8vo, 3*s.* 6*d.*

BOWEN, *H. C., M.A.*—Simple English Poems. English Literature for Junior Classes. In Four Parts. Parts I., II., and III., 6*d.* each, and Part IV., 1*s.*

BRYANT, W. C.—Poems. Red-line Edition. With 24 Illustrations and Portrait of the Author. Crown 8vo, extra, 7*s.* 6*d.*
A Cheap Edition, with Frontispiece. Small crown 8vo, 3*s.* 6*d.*

BYRNNE, E. *Fairfax.*—Milicent : a Poem. Small crown 8vo, 6*s.*

Calderon's Dramas : the Wonder-Working Magician — Life is a Dream—the Purgatory of St. Patrick. Translated by DENIS FLORENCE MACCARTHY. Post 8vo, 10*s.*

Castilian Brothers (The), Chateaubriant, Waldemar: Three Tragedies; and The Rose of Sicily: a Drama. By the Author of "Ginevra," &c. Crown 8vo, 6s.

Chronicles of Christopher Columbus. A Poem in 12 Cantos. By M. D. C. Crown 8vo, 7s. 6d.

CLARKE, *Mary Cowden.*—Honey from the Weed. Verses. Crown 8vo, 7s.

COLOMB, *Colonel.*—The Cardinal Archbishop: a Spanish Legend. In 29 Cancions. Small crown 8vo, 5s.

CONWAY, *Hugh.*—A Life's Idylls. Small crown 8vo, 3s. 6d.

COPPÉE, *Francois.*—L'Exilée. Done into English Verse, with the sanction of the Author, by I. O. L. Crown 8vo, vellum, 5s.

COXHEAD, *Ethel.*—Birds and Babies. Imp. 16mo. With 33 Illustrations. Gilt, 2s. 6d.

David Rizzio, Bothwell, and the Witch Lady. Three Tragedies by the author of "Ginevra," etc. Crown 8vo, 6s.

DAVIE, *G. S., M.D.*—The Garden of Fragrance. Being a complete translation of the Bostán of Sádi from the original Persian into English Verse. Crown 8vo, 7s. 6d.

DAVIES, *T. Hart.*—Catullus. Translated into English Verse. Crown 8vo, 6s.

DE VERE, *Aubrey.*—The Foray of Queen Meave, and other Legends of Ireland's Heroic Age. Small crown 8vo, 5s.

Legends of the Saxon Saints. Small crown 8vo, 6s.

DILLON, *Arthur.*—River Songs and other Poems. With 13 autotype Illustrations from designs by Margery May. Fcap. 4to, cloth extra, gilt leaves, 10s. 6d.

DOBELL, *Mrs. Horace.*—Ethelstone, Eveline, and other Poems. Crown 8vo, 6s.

DOBSON, *Austin.*—Old World Idylls and other Poems. 18mo, cloth extra, gilt tops, 6s.

DOMET, *Alfred.*—Ranolf and Amohia. A Dream of Two Lives. New Edition, Revised. 2 vols. Crown 8vo, 12s.

Dorothy: a Country Story in Elegiac Verse. With Preface. Demy 8vo, 5s.

DOWDEN, *Edward, LL.D.*—Shakspere's Sonnets. With Introduction. Large post 8vo, 7s. 6d.

DOWNTON, *Rev. H., M.A.*—Hymns and Verses. Original and Translated. Small crown 8vo, 3s. 6d.

DUTT, *Toru.*—A Sheaf Gleaned in French Fields. New Edition. Demy 8vo, 10s. 6d.

EDMONDS, E. W.—**Hesperas.** Rhythm and Rhyme. **Crown** 8vo, 4s.

ELDRYTH, Maud.—**Margaret,** and other Poems. Small crown 8vo, 3s. 6d.

ELLIOTT, Ebenezer, The Corn Law Rhymer.—Poems. Edited by his son, the Rev. EDWIN ELLIOTT, of St. John's, Antigua. 2 vols. Crown 8vo, 18s.

English Odes. Selected, with a Critical Introduction by EDMUND W. GOSSE, and a miniature frontispiece by Hamo Thornycroft, A.R.A. Elzevir 8vo, limp parchment antique, 6s. ; vellum, 7s. 6d.

EVANS, Anne.—**Poems and Music.** With Memorial Preface by ANN THACKERAY RITCHIE. Large crown 8vo, 7s.

GOSSE, Edmund W.—**New Poems.** Crown 8vo, 7s. 6d.

GRAHAM, William. **Two Fancies and** other Poems. **Crown** 8vo, 5s.

GRINDROD, Charles. **Plays from English History.** Crown 8vo, 7s. 6d.

GURNEY, Rev. Alfred.—**The Vision of the Eucharist,** and other Poems. Crown 8vo, 5s.

HELLON, H. G.—**Daphnis:** a Pastoral Poem. Small crown 8vo, 3s. 6d.

Herman Waldgrave: a Life's Drama. By the Author of "Ginevra," etc. Crown 8vo, 6s.

HICKEY, E. H.—**A Sculptor,** and other Poems. Small crown 8vo, 5s.

Horati Opera. Edited by F. A. CORNISH, Assistant Master at Eton. With a Frontispiece after a design by L. Alma Tadema, etched by Leopold Lowenstam. Parchment Library Edition, 6s.; vellum, 7s. 6d.

INGHAM, Sarson, C. J.—**Cædmon's Vision, and other Poems.** Small crown 8vo, 5s.

JENKINS, Rev. Canon.—**Alfonso Petrucci,** Cardinal and Conspirator: an Historical Tragedy in Five Acts. Small crown 8vo, 3s. 6d.

KING, Edward.—**Echoes from the Orient.** With Miscellaneous Poems. Small crown 8vo, 3s. 6d.

KING, Mrs. Hamilton.—**The Disciples.** Fifth Edition, with Portrait and Notes. Crown 8vo, 5s.

    A Book of Dreams. Crown 8vo, 5s.

LANG, A.—**XXXII Ballades in Blue China.** Elzevir 8vo, parchment, 5s.

LAWSON, Right Hon. Mr. Justice.—Hymni Usitati Latine Redditi : with other Verses. Small 8vo, parchment, 5*s.*

LEIGH, Arran and Isla.—Bellerophon. Small crown 8vo, 5*s.*

LEIGHTON, Robert.—Records, and other Poems. With Portrait. Small crown 8vo, 7*s.* 6*d.*

Lessings Nathan the Wise. Translated by EUSTACE K. CORBETT. Crown 8vo, 6*s.*

Living English Poets MDCCCLXXXII. With Frontispiece by Walter Crane. Second Edition. Large crown 8vo. Printed on hand-made paper. Parchment, 12*s.,* vellum, 15*s.*

LOCKER, F.—London Lyrics. A New and Cheaper Edition. Small crown 8vo, 2*s.* 6*d.*

Love in Idleness. A Volume of Poems. With an etching by W. B. Scott. Small crown 8vo, 5*s.*

Love Sonnets of Proteus. With Frontispiece by the Author. Elzevir 8vo, 5*s.*

LOWNDES, Henry.—Poems and Translations. Crown 8vo, 6*s.*

LUMSDEN, Lieut.-Col. H. W.—Beowulf : an Old English Poem. Translated into Modern Rhymes. Second Edition. Small crown 8vo, 5*s.*

Lyre and Star. Poems by the Author of "Ginevra," etc. Crown 8vo, 5*s.*

MACLEAN, Charles Donald.—Latin and Greek Verse Translations. Small crown 8vo, 2*s.*

MAGNUSSON, Eirikr, M.A., and PALMER, E. H., M.A.—Johan Ludvig Runeberg's Lyrical Songs, Idylls, and Epigrams. Fcap. 8vo, 5*s.*

M.D.C.—Chronicles of Christopher Columbus. A Poem in Twelve Cantos. Crown 8vo, 7*s.* 6*d.*

MEREDITH, Owen, The Earl of Lytton.—Lucile. New Edition. With 32 Illustrations. 16mo, 3*s.* 6*d.* Cloth extra, gilt edges, 4*s.* 6*d.*

MIDDLETON, The Lady.—Ballads. Square 16mo, 3*s.* 6*d.*

MORICE, Rev. F. D., M.A.—The Olympian and Pythian Odes of Pindar. A New Translation in English Verse. Crown 8vo, 7*s.* 6*d.*

MORRIS, Lewis.—Poetical Works of. New and Cheaper Editions, with Portrait. Complete in 3 vols., 5*s.* each.
Vol. I. contains "Songs of Two Worlds." Vol. II. contains "The Epic of Hades." Vol. III. contains "Gwen" and "The Ode of Life."

D

MORRIS, Lewis—continued.

The Epic of Hades. With 16 Autotype Illustrations, after the Drawings of the late George R. Chapman. 4to, cloth extra, gilt leaves, 25s.

The Epic of Hades. Presentation Edition. 4to, cloth extra, gilt leaves, 10s. 6d.

Ode of Life, The. Fourth Edition. Crown 8vo, 5s.

Songs Unsung. Fcap. 8vo.

MORSHEAD, E. D. A. — **The House of Atreus.** Being the Agamemnon, Libation-Bearers, and Furies of Æschylus. Translated into English Verse. Crown 8vo, 7s.

The Suppliant Maidens of Æschylus. Crown 8vo, 3s. 6d.

NADEN, Constance W.—**Songs and Sonnets of Spring Time.** Small crown 8vo, 5s.

NEWELL, E. J.—**The Sorrows of Simona and Lyrical Verses.** Small crown 8vo, 3s. 6d.

NOAKE, Major R. Compton.—**The Bivouac ; or, Martial Lyrist.** With an Appendix : Advice to the Soldier. Fcap. 8vo, 5s. 6d.

NOEL, The Hon. Roden.—**A Little Child's Monument.** Second Edition. Small crown 8vo, 3s. 6d.

NORRIS, Rev. Alfred.—**The Inner and Outer Life.** Poems. Fcap. 8vo, 6s.

O'HAGAN, John.—**The Song of Roland.** Translated into English Verse. New and Cheaper Edition. Crown 8vo, 5s.

PFEIFFER, Emily.—**Glan Alarch : His Silence and Song : a Poem.** Second Edition. Crown 8vo, 6s.

Gerard's Monument, and other Poems. Second Edition. Crown 8vo, 6s.

Quarterman's Grace, and other Poems. Crown 8vo, 5s.

Poems. Second Edition. Crown 8vo, 6s.

Sonnets and Songs. New Edition. 16mo, handsomely printed and bound in cloth, gilt edges, 4s.

Under the Aspens : Lyrical and Dramatic. With Portrait. Crown 8vo, 6s.

PIKE, Warburton.—**The Inferno of Dante Allighieri.** Demy 8vo, 5s.

POE, Edgar Allan.—**Poems.** With an Essay on his Poetry by ANDREW LANG, and a Frontispiece by Linley Sambourne. Parchment Library Edition, 6s. ; vellum, 7s. 6d.

Rare Poems of the 16th and 17th Centuries. Edited W. J. LINTON. Crown 8vo, 5s.

RHOADES, James.—**The Georgics of Virgil.** Translated into English Verse. Small crown 8vo, 5s.

ROBINSON, A. Mary F.—**A Handful of Honeysuckle.** Fcap. 8vo, 3s. 6d.

   The Crowned Hippolytus. Translated from Euripides. With New Poems. Small crown 8vo, 5s.

SAUNDERS, John.—**Love's Martyrdom.** A Play and Poem. Small crown 8vo, 5s.

Schiller's Mary Stuart. German Text, with English Translation on opposite page by LEEDHAM WHITE. Crown 8vo, 6s.

SCOTT, George F. E.—**Theodora and other Poems.** Small 8vo, 3s. 6d.

SELKIRK, J. B.—**Poems.** Crown 8vo, 7s. 6d.

Shakspere's Sonnets. Edited by EDWARD DOWDEN. With a Frontispiece etched by Leopold Lowenstam, after the Death Mask. Parchment Library Edition, 6s. ; vellum, 7s. 6d.

Shakspere's Works. Complete in 12 Volumes. Parchment Library Edition, 6s. each ; vellum, 7s. 6d. each.

SHAW, W. F., M.A.—**Juvenal, Persius, Martial, and Catullus.** An Experiment in Translation. Crown 8vo, 5s.

SHELLEY, Percy Bysshe.—**Poems Selected from.** Dedicated to Lady Shelley. With Preface by RICHARD GARNETT. Parchment Library Edition, 6s. ; vellum, 7s. 6d.

Six Ballads about King Arthur. Crown 8vo, extra, gilt edges, 3s. 6d.

SLADEN, Douglas B.—**Frithjof and Ingebjorg, and other Poems.** Small crown 8vo, 5s.

TAYLOR, Sir H.—**Works.** Complete in Five Volumes. Crown 8vo, 30s.

   Philip Van Artevelde. Fcap. 8vo, 3s. 6d.

   The Virgin Widow, etc. Fcap. 8vo, 3s. 6d.

   The Statesman. Fcap. 8vo, 3s. 6d.

TENNYSON, Alfred.—Works Complete :—

   The Imperial Library Edition. Complete in 7 vols. Demy 8vo, 10s. 6d. each ; in Roxburgh binding, 12s. 6d. each.

   Author's Edition. In 7 vols. Post 8vo, gilt 43s. 6d. ; or half-morocco, Roxburgh style, 54s.

   Cabinet Edition. 13 vols. Each with Frontispiece. Fcap. 8vo, 2s. 6d. each.

   Cabinet Edition. 13 vols. Complete in handsome Ornamental Case. 35s.

TENNYSON, Alfred—continued.

> **The Royal Edition.** In 1 vol. With 26 Illustrations and Portrait. Extra, bevelled boards, gilt leaves, 21s.
>
> **The Guinea Edition.** Complete in 13 vols. neatly bound and enclosed in box, 21s. ; French morocco or parchment, 31s. 6d.
>
> **Shilling Edition.** In 13 vols. pocket size, 1s. each, sewed.
>
> **The Crown Edition.** Complete in 1 vol. strongly bound, 6s. ; extra gilt leaves, 7s. 6d. ; Roxburgh, half-morocco, 8s. 6d.
>   *⁎*⁎* Can also be had in a variety of other bindings.
>
> **In Memoriam.** With a Miniature Portrait in *eau-forte* by Le Rat, after a Photograph by the late Mrs. Cameron. Parchment Library Edition, 6s. ; vellum, 7s. 6d.
>
> **The Princess.** A Medley. With a Miniature Frontispiece by H. M. Paget, and a Tailpiece in Outline by Gordon Browne. Parchment Library Edition, 6s. ; vellum, 7s. 6d.
>
> Original Editions :—
>
> **Poems.** Small 8vo, 6s.
>
> **Maud, and other Poems.** Small 8vo, 3s. 6d.
>
> **The Princess.** Small 8vo, 3s. 6d.
>
> **Idylls of the King.** Small 8vo, 5s.
>
> **Idylls of the King.** Complete. Small 8vo, 6s.
>
> **The Holy Grail, and other Poems.** Small 8vo, 4s. 6d.
>
> **Gareth and Lynette.** Small 8vo, 3s.
>
> **Enoch Arden, etc.** Small 8vo, 3s. 6d.
>
> **In Memoriam.** Small 8vo, 4s.
>
> **Harold : a Drama.** New Edition. Crown 8vo, 6s.
>
> **Queen Mary : a Drama.** New Edition. Crown 8vo, 6s.
>
> **The Lover's Tale.** Fcap. 8vo, 3s. 6d.
>
> **Ballads, and other Poems.** Small 8vo, 5s.
>
> **Selections from the above Works.** Super royal 16mo, 3s. 6d. ; gilt extra, 4s.
>
> **Songs from the above Works.** 16mo, 2s. 6d.

Tennyson for the Young and for Recitation. Specially arranged. Fcap. 8vo, 1s. 6d.

The Tennyson Birthday Book. Edited by EMILY SHAKESPEAR. 32mo, limp, 2s. ; extra, 3s.
>   *⁎*⁎* A superior Edition, printed in red and black, on antique paper, specially prepared. Small crown 8vo, extra, gilt leaves, 5s. ; and in various calf and morocco bindings.

THORNTON, L. M.—The Son of Shelomith. Small crown 8vo, 3s. 6d.

TODHUNTER, Dr. J.—Laurella, and other Poems. Crown 8vo, 6s. 6d.

    Forest Songs. Small crown 8vo, 3s. 6d.

    The True Tragedy of Rienzi : a Drama. 3s. 6d.

    Alcestis : a Dramatic Poem. Extra fcap. 8vo, 5s.

    A Study of Shelley. Crown 8vo, 7s.

Translations from Dante, Petrarch, Michael Angelo, and Vittoria Colonna. Fcap. 8vo, 7s. 6d.

TURNER, Rev. C. Tennyson.—Sonnets, Lyrics, and Translations. Crown 8vo, 4s. 6d.

    Collected Sonnets, Old and New. With Prefatory Poem by ALFRED TENNYSON; also some Marginal Notes by S. T. COLERIDGE, and a Critical Essay by JAMES SPEDDING. Fcap. 8vo, 7s. 6d.

WALTERS, Sophia Lydia.—A Dreamer's Sketch Book. With 21 Illustrations by Percival Skelton, R. P. Leitch, W. H. J. Boot, and T. R. Pritchett. Engraved by J. D. Cooper. Fcap. 4to, 12s. 6d.

WEBSTER, Augusta.—In a Day : a Drama. Small crown 8vo, 2s. 6d.

Wet Days. By a Farmer. Small crown 8vo, 6s.

WILKINS, William.—Songs of Study. Crown 8vo, 6s.

WILLIAMS, J.—A Story of Three Years, and other Poems. Small crown 8vo, 3s. 6d.

YOUNGS, Ella Sharpe.—Paphus, and other Poems. Small crown 8vo, 3s. 6d.

WORKS OF FICTION IN ONE VOLUME.

BANKS, Mrs. G. L.—God's Providence House. New Edition. Crown 8vo, 3s. 6d.

HARDY, Thomas.—A Pair of Blue Eyes. Author of "Far from the Madding Crowd." New Edition. Crown 8vo, 6s.

    The Return of the Native. New Edition. With Frontispiece. Crown 8vo, 6s.

INGELOW, Jean.—Off the Skelligs : a Novel. With Frontispiece. Second Edition. Crown 8vo, 6s.

MACDONALD, G.—Castle Warlock. A Novel. New and Cheaper Edition. Crown 8vo, 6s.

MACDONALD, G.—continued.

Malcolm. With Portrait of the Author engraved on Steel. Sixth Edition. Crown 8vo, 6s.

The Marquis of Lossie. Fourth Edition. With Frontispiece. Crown 8vo, 6s.

St. George and St. Michael. Third Edition. With Frontispiece. Crown 8vo, 6s.

PALGRAVE, W. Gifford.—Hermann Agha: an Eastern Narrative. Third Edition. Crown 8vo, 6s.

SHAW, Flora L.—Castle Blair; a Story of Youthful Lives. New and Cheaper Edition. Crown 8vo, 3s. 6d.

STRETTON, Hesba.—Through a Needle's Eye: a Story. New and Cheaper Edition, with Frontispiece. Crown 8vo, 6s.

TAYLOR, Col. Meadows, C.S.I., M.R.I.A.—Seeta: a Novel. New and Cheaper Edition. With Frontispiece. Crown 8vo, 6s.

Tippoo Sultaun: a Tale of the Mysore War. New Edition, with Frontispiece. Crown 8vo, 6s.

Ralph Darnell. New and Cheaper Edition. With Frontispiece. Crown 8vo, 6s.

A Noble Queen. New and Cheaper Edition. With Frontispiece. Crown 8vo, 6s.

The Confessions of a Thug. Crown 8vo, 6s.

Tara: a Mahratta Tale. Crown 8vo, 6s.

Within Sound of the Sea. New and Cheaper Edition, with Frontispiece. Crown 8vo, 6s.

BOOKS FOR THE YOUNG.

Brave Men's Footsteps. A Book of Example and Anecdote for Young People. By the Editor of "Men who have Risen." With 4 Illustrations by C. Doyle. Eighth Edition. Crown 8vo, 3s. 6d.

COXHEAD, Ethel.—Birds and Babies. Imp. 16mo. With 33 Illustrations. Cloth gilt, 2s. 6d.

DAVIES, G. Christopher.—Rambles and Adventures of our School Field Club. With 4 Illustrations. New and Cheaper Edition. Crown 8vo, 3s. 6d.

EDMONDS, Herbert.—Well Spent Lives: a Series of Modern Biographies. New and Cheaper Edition. Crown 8vo, 3s. 6d.

EVANS, Mark.—**The Story of our Father's Love**, told to Children. Fourth and Cheaper Edition of Theology for Children. With 4 Illustrations. Fcap. 8vo, 1s. 6d.

JOHNSON, Virginia W.—**The Catskill Fairies.** Illustrated by Alfred Fredericks. 5s.

MAC KENNA, S. J.—**Plucky Fellows.** A Book for Boys. With 6 Illustrations. Fifth Edition. Crown 8vo, 3s. 6d.

REANEY, Mrs. G. S.—**Waking and Working;** or, From Girlhood to Womanhood. New and Cheaper Edition. With a Frontispiece. Crown 8vo, 3s. 6d.

Blessing and Blessed: a Sketch of Girl Life. New and Cheaper Edition. Crown 8vo, 3s. 6d.

Rose Gurney's Discovery. A Book for Girls. Dedicated to their Mothers. Crown 8vo, 3s. 6d.

English Girls: Their Place and Power. With Preface by the Rev. R. W. Dale. Fourth Edition. Fcap. 8vo, 2s. 6d.

Just Anyone, and other Stories. Three Illustrations. Royal 16mo, 1s. 6d.

Sunbeam Willie, and other Stories. Three Illustrations. Royal 16mo, 1s. 6d.

Sunshine Jenny, and other Stories. Three Illustrations. Royal 16mo, 1s. 6d.

STOCKTON, Frank R.—**A Jolly Fellowship.** With 20 Illustrations. Crown 8vo, 5s.

STORR, Francis, and TURNER, Hawes.—**Canterbury Chimes;** or, Chaucer Tales retold to Children. With 6 Illustrations from the Ellesmere MS. Second Edition. Fcap. 8vo, 3s. 6d.

STRETTON, Hesba.—**David Lloyd's Last Will.** With 4 Illustrations. New Edition. Royal 16mo, 2s. 6d.

Tales from Ariosto Re-told for Children. By a Lady. With 3 Illustrations. Crown 8vo, 4s. 6d.

WHITAKER, Florence.—**Christy's Inheritance.** A London Story. Illustrated. Royal 16mo, 1s. 6d.

PRINTED BY WILLIAM CLOWES AND SONS, LIMITED, LONDON AND BECCLES.

www.ingramcontent.com/pod-product-compliance
Lightning Source LLC
Chambersburg PA
CBHW032007060726
47497CB00017B/2368